MOONSHINE

Part 1 of the River Bottom Saga

DEBRA FULLER

STARDUST PUBLISHING

Onalaska, TX

This book is a work of fiction. Any person, character, places, and incidents are a result of the author's imagination or are used fictionally. Any resemblance to actual events, locales, or persons, living or dead is coincidental.

www.debrafuller.com

Stardust Publishing LLC
Onalaska, Texas
StardustPublishingLLC@gmail.com

Ordering Information: Please contact the publisher regarding quantity sales.

Printed in the United States of America.

Cover and book design by Michelle Brodeur, @eebooWORX (mich-bro.myportfolio.com)

ISBN: 978-0999861523 (paperback)
ISBN: 0999861516 (ebook)

First Edition

0 9 8 7 6 5 4 3 2 1

In memory of Bobby "Lobo" Fuller.
A wonderfully prolific storyteller and the
most unconditionally loving Daddy a girl could ever have.

Acknowledgements

Lauren Weems Fuller thank you, from the bottom of my heart, for being my champion helping me drive this work to completion.

To my many friends who have encouraged me throughout the course of this experience cheering me on with your wonderful moral support. . . I thank you.

Karen Kleinpeter Moss thank you for providing your cajun dialect expertise for Joe. I could not have brought him appropriately to life without you.

Michelle Brodeur, @eebooWORX (mich-bro.myportfolio.com), thank you for bringing my story to life through the amazing work you executed on the cover of this book.

Jennifer Kiely thank you for your editorial eyes and valuable input.

Texas Tea Formed

Son of a Bitch! You wouldn't believe what happened down here in the river bottom the other day. It's the biggest shit pile that has come to this neck of the woods in a long time. That damn Ouida Mae did it again. She got herself wrapped up in an illegal venture that touched everyone in the county. Although the community appeared stunned at what happened, the grapevine had connected them all to the events as they unfolded.

Those not drawn to this part of East Texas would ever understand the allure it has for us locals. City slickers would be in fear for their own lives venturing down here. They would never survive the mosquitoes, snakes, feral hogs and occasional nutria rat. Driving down here at night, one might imagine they are hearing a banjo playing that ominous song from "Deliverance". Those same folks would be stretching their necks out their car windows keeping an eye out for a spook or two fearing they could be pulled into Old Man Pinkie's swamp by a monster alligator. We folk down here, however, love this place due to the natural surroundings and peaceful calm it can bring. The Trinity River runs through the river bottom winding down from Lake Livingston to this side of the county. Teaming with wildlife it provides a watering hole for the local bald eagle family, egrets, blue heron, deer and alike. Great old homesteads exist echoing the tales of stories long gone by passed down from generations of farmers, share croppers and ranchers. Wrapped around each country home exists a porch where folks find time to rest a spell, celebrate and solve the world's problems. We locals consider this area a hiding place, a place of solitude, a place to fly under the radar and definitely a place for entrepreneurship of the mysterious kind. Overall it's typically a quiet place to spend your life but every now and again the cast iron skillet gets stirred and the spice flies.

So it all began one June afternoon when Tater's daddy, Robert Murphy, started up an oil recycling business for her. Murphy is the pillar of our local township. He owns quite a bit of property in Shepherd, Texas and throughout San Jacinto County. He spent his entire childhood here and has quite a few lifelong friends as a result. Everyone looks up to and respects him. He knows everything about business dealings in the county and if you want to get the latest, all you have to do is pop a few quarters in the Coke cooler, open a bottle and sit a spell on one of the tractor seats welded to the posts on the local feed store porch. Sooner or later he'll share what he knows with you. He is your typical East Texas businessman. He's always noodling a business idea and willing to talk about it. When he speaks, his voice booms a mile away and makes the most skittish yard cat sit up and take notice. Folks say he made his fortune in Houston during the oil heyday. Because he grew up in Shepherd, he decided to settle down here after selling his business for a fortune.

He loves his daughter Tater and wants her to be as successful as he has been. Sure, she graduated from Shepherd High School but never had a desire to go to college. She was one of those types who felt you didn't have to go to some big school to do well. She felt hard work, a bit of sweat and a strong determination would get you where you wanted to go. Fortunately, her daddy felt the same. He explored many business ideas that would fit well in the county and decided to incorporate Texas Tea Refinery for his daughter. His idea was to set up the containers and machinery to process used oil and recycle it into useable products for statewide distribution. He had contacts all over the state that were willing to do business with he and Tater. His good ole boy oil connections were crucial to the success of the business. After setting up the business plan, he invited his daughter over for dinner and talked through the idea with her.

Tater entered her Daddy's house and walked past the hat rack adorned by his Stetson surrounded with a turquoise band. Tater could smell his chemtrail of brut wafting through the house. Murphy's voice boomed.

"How you doin' there Tater baby?"

"I'm as stiff as those creases down the front of your

Wranglers there Daddy. Just wrapped up a five mile run and feel like my legs are about to fall out from under me."

Murphy pulled a comb out of his pocked and ran it through his shock of white hair as a matter of habit. Tater knew this action well.

"What's goin' on in that brain of yours Daddy?"

"Tater, I believe this business is well suited for you. It will start out as a small operation yet in no time I am certain you will expand this company into multiple states."

"Daddy, I like the structure. It's definitely something I could manage on my own to begin with. Plus, this will be all mine. Something I can be proud of."

"I have only one caveat Tater."

"What's that Daddy?"

"I will have audit control of the books and will be reviewing them on a quarterly basis. I'll also throw in a surprise audit here and there to keep you, my red-headed wild child, on your toes."

"Not a problem at all Daddy. I'll make you proud!"

He and Tater shook on the agreement and they began sourcing the location, materials and equipment to get the facility up and running.

Murphy invited his business partners to the grand opening of the operation. He had them all come down one weekend for a trail ride and bar-b-cue as a thank you for their commitment to contributing financially to the business. They all arrived on a steamy hot August Saturday morning and met Murphy at the town mercantile. One of the local ranchers brought horses, bridled with tack, for everyone. It was an event unlike anything that had gone on in the river bottom. Murphy mounted his horse and waived everyone to do the same.

"Welcome everyone! Let's get a move on!"

The group of riders traveled east down FM 1127 towards Mrs. Cotton's old home site. She owned 500 acres of East Texas farmland lined with a willow orchard and two huge lakes. The property was occupied by livestock including cows, horses, alpacas and ostrich. Murphy was able to talk her out of twenty acres closest to FM 1127 that would allow for plenty of room to expand the business, yet country enough to keep Tater happy. As the group rode up on the site, their eyes brightened to the display before them. A huge welded metal sign loomed over the entryway to the property displaying the words "Texas Tea, LLC." In the yard were parked four tankers with the same logo emblazoned on each side.

As everyone dismounted from their horses, they jumped back surprised by a screech coming through the entry way to the facility. A fire engine red Dodge Ram Hemi dually diesel came to a halt sending gravel and dirt flying everywhere. "I'm not ready to make nice" blared the Dixie Chicks from the windows as Tater

Murphy lunged out of the driver's side of the pickup. Mr. Hanes, one of Murphy's long-time padna's, walked over to Tater.

"Tater girl, you definitely are much prettier than your daddy. However, you should think about putting on a few more pounds before a strong wind comes and carries you off."

"Is that right Mr. Hanes?"

Tater removed her Texas Tea, LLC ball cap, pulled her fiery red braided pony tail through the snapback of the cap and repositioned it on her head. Her bright green eyes glared out from under the tightly rolled brim towards Mr. Hanes and she threw him a pearly white grin. She headed towards her daddy whistling her siren call and waved at the onlookers.

"Hi-dee y'all! How y'all like the new digs?"

Tater hopped up on the porch, brushed off her Levi's 501s and kicked the dust off her shit kickers. Most of the folks present had known Tater since she was born. They loved her like they loved her daddy. At one point or another, most of them became a surrogate to her after her mother passed. Her daddy had been running with these guys and gals since way back in the day. Their bonds were strong and true.

Tater proceeded to give everyone a tour of the facilities. A ranch style one story office building was the cornerstone of the property surrounded by a wrap-around porch which held a few rocking chairs. It had a log cabin facade and was covered with a brick red Muller roof and overhang. The inside of the building contained a meeting room, lunch room, computer server room, men's and women's facilities as well as Tater's office. The office was accented with a huge cherrywood desk, the front of which was hand carved with hummingbirds and wolves against a forest backdrop. Atop the desk was a welded nameplate bearing the title "Tater Murphy, CEO." Her favorite office accoutrements also resided on the desk including a 17-inch MacBook Pro, a jar full of cherry sours, another full of jawbreakers and a third full of Atkinson Candy Peanut Butter Bars. Behind the desk was a Herman Miller Aeron Chair decked out with lumbar support and leather trim. Brown wooden shutters accented the windows and a couple of big fat Pottery Barn Buster leather chairs were placed opposite the desk.

A huge metal storage barn was located out back alongside a brand new processing tank that would process and contain the refined oils rendered from the sludge output of local refineries. There was an additional backup unit situated next to it which would be used in the event there were problems with the main processor or there was a need to expand production over the next few months. It was quite a setup containing the latest technology this side of East Texas had ever seen. The server room held the brains behind the processors and had every bell and whistle one could think of to control not only the units but the security to the entire yard.

Excitement filled the air. Everyone knew this was a new

day for Tater and her daddy. Murphy stood up on the porch and looked over the crowd. His voice boomed over the excitement.

"Now you all know that we aren't just here for food and fun. I want you to know that Tater and I feel this fantastic new business is going to be a hit for generations to come. We want to thank each of you, from the bottom of our hearts, for taking on the challenge as angel investors for Texas Tea, LLC. We have such a belief that this place is going to grow by leaps and bounds and we will eventually set up similar operations in just about every state across the country. However, for now, we will stick to the business at hand and get this thing started and profitable before we make any bigger moves."

Murphy winked at the crowd and they all applauded in agreement. With the tip of Murphy's hat, servers came out of the office holding trays stacked with shots of Gentleman Jack. A four-piece bluegrass band started playing on the porch. Murphy raised a glass to those present. He turned towards his daughter and proclaimed, "To Tater and Texas Tea, LLC!"

Everyone echoed the sentiment and settled down to an afternoon of bar-b-cue, storytelling, drinking and song.

CUEBALL

Tater was a smart business gal like her daddy but she didn't have a lick of sense when it came to the company she kept. She had a childhood friend she ran with throughout her formative years, Johnny Whitehead. Tater calls him Cueball on account of he is as bald as the day he was born. He is truly a nice guy at heart but never had a good business acumen about him. Cueball had seen his fair share of delinquency. He spent enough of his free time in the county jail. His specialty was stealing copper to support his hooch drinking habit. Cueball could charm the socks off a cranky old maid. Although he and Tater weren't intimately involved, they had a brother-sister connection. Tater always felt the need to keep tabs on him making sure he stayed out of trouble. Otherwise, he would get himself into a bind and come running to Tater for help.

Tater, deciding that she would need help with her new business, thought it best to get Cueball on the payroll to keep him out of trouble and supplied with a bit of cash flow to meet his needs. Not long after picking up the phone and asking him to come on over, Tater could hear the whine of an old Chevy Nova rolling into the parking lot. The fan belt, always loose, caused a high pitched whirr as it clunked to a stop. The car backfired and stuttered with a puff of black smoke.

There was a knock on her office door.

"Come on in Cue."

Cue walked in and flashed a brown Redman smile towards Tater.

"God, Cue. When are you going to stop chewin' that nasty stuff? The least you can do is wipe that brown slobber out of the corner of your mouth!"

Cueball plopped down in the big leather chair and threw his muddy Skechers on her desk.

"Cue! What the hell are you doing dragging your muddy ass feet up on my desk?"

Cueball quickly removed his feet and wiped the desk with his wife beater T.

"Sorry! What have you got goin' on here? This is quite a setup your old daddy hooked you up with!"

"Yep, Cue, this is an exciting business we've started and I would like you to be my right hand padna around here. Interested?"

"Depends, Tater."

"Depends on what, Cue?"

"Well, how much you gonna pay me? How many days a week do I need to work? What in the world do you need me for? I'm awful busy with the stuff I'm doin'."

"Busy huh?" Tater threw a sarcastic grin at Cue.

Tater explained to him that she needed him to help her accept the incoming sludge, run it through the processors and fill tankers five days a week. He would be paid a competitive starting wage with a review and potential for a raise in ninety days. The only caveat is he would have to ditch his current duds and wear a uniform to present better to the customers coming in. Tater took Cueball on a tour of the facilities. Cueball couldn't believe the setup and the equipment it took to get such a business operational. They returned to the office.

"What do you say Cue? Are you in?"

"Hell yes I'm in! This is gonna be great!"

Tater handed him a couple of hangers with pants and shirts as well as a pair of steel-toed boots and a baseball cap.

"Why don't you go try a set on and let's see if those pants are too long for those nubby legs you walk on?"

Cueball disappeared into the bathroom. A few minutes later, he walked through the door as the legs of his new Wranglers swished between his thighs. He struck a GQ pose and motioned to the "Texas Tea LLC" patch that rested above the left pocket of his Dickey's shirt. He tipped his company ball cap off his head and bowed to Tater.

"How do I look madam?"

Tater laughed out loud and nodded her head in satisfaction.

"Cue, you best watch out with those boots. They can get you into a lot of trouble."

Cue demonstrated a pride about his appearance although he complained about the itchy new clothes.

"You clean up real good Cue. The girls better watch out now!"

Cueball smiled his half tooth grin and his face burned red as the chewing tobacco dripped out of the corner of his mouth.

Cueball wasn't sure about this entire refining thing so he asked Tater to explain more. She explained there was an untapped market to recycle used oil for other products out in the marketplace. Cueball scratched his head and asked her to break it down "more simply please."

"So we take all that oil waste that has been collected at service stations and oil changing shops. We then process and clean it up to be used again as passenger motor oil, lubricants, hydraulics, you name it! It's a great way to get another bang for your buck and definitely is a great 'recycling' alternative."

Tater popped a jawbreaker in her mouth as she saw a light go off in Cueball's brain once she explained what the refined product could be used for. Cueball looked at her and the questions fired off.

"So, they bring in the crappy stuff and you clean it up and sell it like new again?"

Tater nodded her head yes.

"I'm willing to make a go at it and hope to learn more about how the process works. Now I get how you came up with that thar name 'Texas Tea, LLC'. . .just like the Beverly Freakin' Hillbillies!"

Tater laughed so hard the jawbreaker shot out of her mouth and hit Cueball square on his forehead leaving a red sticky mark.

"When can I start?"

"Be here at seven tomorrow morning and we'll get things going."

Sisters From Another Mister

Cueball hung with another gal by the name of Ouida Mae Lawless. The pronunciation of her name sounds more like "Weed-a". The beauty of her name is nowhere near the resounding screech of her voice which makes the hair stand up on the back of your neck. When she opens that foul mouth of hers, you can hear it all over the county. Deep like a man's voice but gurgly like she's been drowning in her own spit. She is a sight to be seen and heard. Ouida has a reputation as the bitch of the county and most folk try not to have anything to do with her.

Ouida runs a local icehouse and owns a fair share of property in the county on account she inherited the land from her folks. Cueball does odd jobs for Ouida and rents a small Shasta vintage travel trailer, parked behind her bar. She thinks she has rule and reign over just about everybody in town because her poor deceased daddy used to be the mayor. Ouida has no problem threatening newcomers. If those folks don't know she's the town bully, they'll find out soon enough. For some reason, most people simply turn a blind eye to her antics and consider it just her crazy ass ways. Honestly, she is generally harmless. Ask other folks in this county, however, and they would show you a gun with her name carved on it.

Cueball walked into Ouida's icehouse. He jumped back at the sight of Ouida's hair sitting on top of her head looking like a rooster's shock, as bleached blonde as a bottle of Clairol No. 9 could get it.

"Can I help you?" asked Ouida as she looked up.

Her crack-toothed mouth just about hit the bar counter when she realized it was Cueball.

"What the hell happened to you, you Sonofabitch?"

Ouida slip slapped in her flip flops towards Cue pulling her cutoff jean shorts out of her backside.

"This here's my new uniform as I'm gunna be workin' fer Tater."

"Huh, let's see how long that lasts."

Cueball's expression changed to a darkness that Ouida had never seen on him.

"You just don't want anyone to do well in this here county but you, you old fuckin' bitch! I'll show you!"

Cueball stormed out of the icehouse madder than a rattlesnake backed into a corner.

Ouida looked over at Coon-Ass Joe.

"Can you believe that? Cue's got a real J-O-B! I believe Hell is freezing over this very minute!"

Coon-Ass Joe looked at her with bloodshot eyes and nodded in agreement.

Ouida wasn't clear on what Tater's new business was and decided to inquire on the local party line aka Dwanna Crabb. Dwanna is Ouida's best friend. Probably because no other woman in the county, or person for that matter, wanted to have anything to do with her on a personal level. Dwanna, one of the local Holy Rollers, is the party line to Polk County. In other words, you don't need to call anyone except Dwanna for the latest gossip in town. That's where she and Ouida fit together like stink on shit. Dwanna has the scoop and Ouida goes after it like a dog smelling another's butt. Dwanna had a heart for Ouida. She felt that if she stayed close to Ouida, one day Ouida would fall in love with Jesus Christ himself. Ouida knew of Dwanna's intentions but didn't let that get in the way of their gossipy friendship. They were definitely a match made in Heaven.

Ouida rang Dwanna up at home. Her voicemail sang through the phone.

"Hallelujah! You have reached Dwanna! I'm probably at church or something and can't get to the phone right now. So, leave a message and I'll call you back. Don't forget. . .Jesus Loves You and I do too!"

Ouida slammed her phone down on the receiver, picked it up again and called Dwanna on her cellphone. This time Dwanna answered.

"Hello Sister!"

"Where are you Dwanna? I need to talk to you!"

"Oh, is everything OK precious one?"

"I'm interested in knowing more about Mr. Murphy's daughter's new business!"

"Oh, Ouida, you mean sweet Tater?"

"Yes, can I come over?"

"Sure, drop by my house for coffee and cake around three this afternoon."

"I'll be by at three sharp!"

Ouida slammed the phone down.

Dwanna had been handling the church bake sale table in front of McMann's grocery store all day. The ladies of the congregation all pitched in and made a ton of desserts to raise funds for their quilting circle. Dwanna made one of her favorites — chocolate peanut butter pineapple pecan upside down cake. It looked like a pile of shit but was mesmerizing enough to the locals that every last slice of it was bought up and eaten before they even reached their cars. Dwanna was pleased to see hers was one of the favorites again. Her shift, over at two, gave her enough time to run home, put a pot of Folger's on and set the table for afternoon conversation. She loved having Ouida over. She knew she was sent from Heaven to help save Ouida's soul and every opportunity she got to spend time with her was well spent for the Kingdom.

Dwanna laid out a lovely white laced tablecloth on her kitchen table. She topped it with her favorite coffee cups and saucers decorated with little lambs. She placed a double chocolate coffee cake on the table knowing that Ouida wouldn't be able to pass it up. She took a moment to sit down at the table and decompress. She leaned on her elbows, rested her face in her hands and prayed a little prayer.

"Dear Lord, guide me in my conversation with Ouida today. I know she is difficult, cantankerous, and potty-mouthed. But Jesus, I do know that you love her as one of your precious children. Help me be a light to her today. In Jesus' Name, Amen."

Just as she was finishing up her prayer she was startled by a bang on her screen door.

"Are you OK!" cried Ouida.

Dwanna motioned Ouida to come on in. She reached up and adjusted a pin in her braided bun to keep it from cascading down her backside. Dwanna towered over Ouida yet had no issue with throwing her lanky arms around her and giving her a big bear hug. Ouida resisted, wrestling from Dwanna's grasp.

"Love your 'Smile Jesus Loves You' t-shirt Dwanna. Were'd you get that? Goodwill?"

"Now Ouida, you know me too well don't ya?"

Dwanna motioned to the table.

"Have a seat while I go grab the coffee."

She poured both she and Ouida a cup.

"Cream or sugar?"

Ouida raised her hand and shook her head no, pulling a small airplane bottle of Jack Black out of her pocket and pouring it in the coffee. Dwanna tried to hide her disdain at Ouida's need to accentuate everything she drank with alcohol but Ouida could see it in her eyes.

"Just a little nip to calm my nerves, it's been an interesting day."

"Well, Ouida, tell me about your day."

"Cue came into the bar all dressed up in his new uniform. Walkin' around like a fuckin' peacock as if he was bigger than shit or somethin' like that. He then proceeded to inform me that he was goin' to work for Tater Murphy at that new erl thing she is doin'."

Dwanna could tell this upset her greatly. Ouida's face started to turn beet red.

"I had him doin' all kinds of jobs for me and he didn't have the decency to ask me if I minded that he go work with Tater too!"

"What are you going to do without Cue's help?"

"I have a right mind to kick him off my property and get Coon-Ass Joe to help out from now on. He might be a drunk but at least he is fuckin' reliable. Dwanna, tell me what you know about that new business Tater's daddy got her all set up in."

"Well, you know that daddy of hers has so much money he doesn't know what to do with it. We have tried for ages to get him to join the church because we could use another good benefactor like him to contribute to church growth. But, that never happened. I'm not sure if he has a personal relationship with Jesus Christ or what so we just keep praying for him."

Ouida gave Dwanna her "who gives a fuck" look but waited for her to continue.

"Mr. Murphy wants Tater to be successful. He knows one day he won't be here forever to help her out so the important thing for him was to start up this oil refining business for her to run. He called in a lot of his old oil buddies and asked them to contribute to the start-up and get Tater off and running. So, they all did. Had a great big party and everything! I heard they were drinking whiskey all night long and shooting off their pistols like they were back in the old West days. They had hookers and pole dancers and everything for those rich old folk. I know Jesus was not happy about all that going on."

"Hookers huh?" Ouida laughed so hard and raspy she almost choked causing Dwanna to ponder whether she was going to have to do mouth to mouth on her. Ouida motioned her to continue.

"Well, after all the partying was done and the dust settled, Mr. Murphy handed the keys to the business over to Tater. Now its' Tater's turn to bring in the customers, hire her staff and start making money. Of course Mr. Murphy is going to keep an eye her books on account of their business arrangement. But he's going to give all other control of the business over to Tater."

"What on God's green earth does Tater want with a bunch of erl? It's one thing to have a daddy who made it big in the business but why in the hell does she want to start drilling?"

"Now Ouida, Tater ain't going to be drilling for oil. She's going to be taking already used oil, cleaning it up and reselling it to companies who use recycled oil."

"So she's now a tree hugger or some shit like that? She thinks she's gonna become rich off recyclin' old crappy motor erl and sellin' it on the black market to make a profit?"

"She's doing this all legit Ouida. The business plan was put together by her daddy and his old buddies and it's clean as a whistle. However, we will have to see how she pulls this off down here in the river bottom."

"I just can't see why she decided to take my Cueball away from me! I need him desperately to help me out around my properties and icehouse. Dwanna, what in the world am I to do?"

"Don't you think Cueball needs something a bit more stable? You don't think he might need something more that might actually keep him out of trouble for once? Don't you see this as being a really good thing for him Ouida?"

Ouida shook her head no. She had always had Cueball under her thumb. The name of her game was manipulation, getting her claws into men and persuading them to do her dirty work. She was a witch in sheep's clothing.

"Still, I'm gonna need to find someone else to help out. He is really puttin' me in a fuckin' bind. In fact, I'm gonna go ahead and kick him off my damn property since he won't be workin' exclusively for me any longer."

"Do what you think you need to do Ouida. The Lord has his ways for people around here and Cueball is definitely in his sights. Speakin' of the Lord Ouida, we are having a square dance down at the community center in September to raise funds for the county quilting bee to make more quilts for our area service men and women. Wanted to know if you would like to come? I hear there will be a few handsome, well-off men there."

"Can't make it Dwanna. Got lots going on that a square dance can't pull me away from."

The ladies continued to catch up on the local gossip, drink coffee and eat cake for another hour. Dwanna wrapped up the remainder of the cake for Ouida as she got up to leave. She gave Ouida a big hug.

"God Bless you Sister. . .have a safe drive home and I'll talk to you soon!"

Cueball's First Day

"What the hell!"

The buzzer on Cueball's alarm clock startled him right out of bed. Signaling him to get up for his first day of work. Cueball wasn't the kind of guy to rise early. He was more of a mid-day person. However, he was determined to prove to Tater that he could do the job and do it well. The voices in his head kept telling him he was a no good shit for nothing bastard. He would never make anything of himself. What did he think he was doing getting up and going to a real job? Cueball shook the voices out of his head and jumped into the shower. Ten minutes later he was sputtering north down US 59 and turning east onto FM 1127 towards Texas Tea, LLC. Tater could hear him coming about a mile away. She was excited to have him join her in the new venture.

"Cue! What in the world are you doing wearing those nasty Skechers?"

"Oh, right. Be right back!"

Cueball ran out to his car and immediately changed into his new work boots before entering her office.

"I didn't want to get them dirty before my first day of work."

"Good thinking Cue!"

Tater took him on a tour of the grounds once more to reacquaint him with the layout. First the office and break room, then over to the server room which really appeared to be more of a glorified closet filled with computer stuff. It went way over Cueball's head. They went outside and around back where the processor was housed.

"See that trap over there Cue? That's where we pour what I call the 'sludge' in, flip this switch and the machine basically does the work for us and spills the final product out into those large vats. Basically, you'll be responsible for emptying the sludge from the trucks into the tanks and kicking off the processors. When the other trucks come in to haul out the 'Tea' you'll hook them up to the vats and flip another switch which is calibrated to fill the entire tanker. Now, what you need to understand is those trucks coming in with the sludge are not owned by Texas Tea. They are simply selling us their sludge for a wholesale profit. The trucks that you are filling up with the refined tea, well, those are ours."

She pointed over to the waiting zone and Cueball saw one of the tankers decked out shiny silver with a gigantic Texas Tea, LLC logo stretched across its length including the company's website and phone number. He couldn't believe how much money went into the operation and how much Tater possibly paid for the tankers.

"You didn't skimp on a damn thing did you Tater?"

Tater shook her head no.

Cueball noticed there was an extra backup processing unit that wasn't in operation yet. He looked at Tater inquisitively.

"What is that for?"

"Backup, in case of electrical failure on the current unit or future expansion of the operation or both."

"Yeah, you definitely thought of everything! What about all that computer equipment you have in there? What is that for?"

"The servers housed in the office are tied to both the company website as well as the operation of the equipment and property security. However, the same data and operations are stored in what you would call a 'Cloud' in the event something catastrophic happens with the servers on site."

Cueball, once again, shook his head in sheer amazement.

"So look here. We get our first sludge trucks coming in this morning. You and I will hook the trucks up, flip the switch and the sludge will vacuum out. After that, we send the trucks on their merry way and turn the processor on. It'll take a full twenty-four hours to refine it into reusable oil. So then tomorrow, you hook up one of our tankers, flip another switch that will expel the oil into the tanker and ready it for delivery. You understand that Cue? We can take upwards of four sludge deliveries a day which will convert to one tanker output. Weekly, we can average five tanker deliveries based on the equipment we have in place currently."

Cueball was actually excited about what he was going to be doing for once.

"So how many of these here processors you expecting to add in the next few years?"

"That's definitely something to be determined at a later date. However, I would like to add one more in the next three to six months max. I'm working with Daddy's padnas and their contacts to build up the business. However, this is a darn good start. I have a full invoicing system to pay our sludge vendors and to receive payment from our refining clients. Once we get the hang of everything and start establishing more clientele, I'll probably hire a salesperson to build the business even further. For now, the company staff consists of me, a couple of tanker drivers and my Logistics Manager."

"Logistics Manager? Who is that?"

"Why that's you, you dumbass!"

"Logistics Manager, ain't that the shit." Cueball whispered.

Right about then the clang of a huge diesel engine turned into the lot. Tater looked up, waved and said, "Hey Ricky!" She then looked at Cueball and exclaimed, "Our first official customer, let's get on it!"

Tater and Cueball worked the discharge of the sludge and flipped the refining switch within the hour. Cueball couldn't believe how simple the entire process was. Tater took Ricky into the office, printed him a receipt and sent the electronic payment to his boss in Tyler, Texas. She also gave Ricky a Texas Tea, LLC ball cap as a sign of appreciation and, of course, free advertising.

"See ya next week Ricky!" hollered Tater as Ricky hopped back into his rig.

"It was great meeting you Cue!" Ricky waived. As he drove off he hit his horn which gave a little Dixie whistle as he headed back to the main highway. Tater and Cueball both looked at each other and died laughing.

Three additional deliveries came in that day and Cueball promptly discharged the sludge into the processor. Cueball then flipped the switch on the processing unit and kicked off their first official recycle round.

Tater slapped Cueball on the back and said, "This deserves a great early dinner for us. Let's go Cue!"

She and Cueball hopped into Tater's truck and sped off to Sallie Jean's diner in town.

Sallie Jean, Tater and Cueball all grew up together attending the same schools, going to the same church and getting whooped by each other's momma a time or two. Sallie Jean peered out the diner window excited to see Tater dropping by the diner that evening. Tater and Cueball stepped inside the diner and gave

Sallie Jean a wave. Sallie Jean is a voluptuous gal standing about five foot two. Her head was covered with ringlets of the softest golden hair reminiscent of Shirley Temple. Her voice was sweet and welcoming. The big chubby rosy grin on her face would melt the heart of any hard-ass.

"Hi Cue! What you doin' hanging around with the likes of this here Tater? It's been quite a while since I've seen you. What have you been doing with yourself?"

"Ah shoot Sallie Jean. I've been here and there trying to stay out of trouble. It's really good to see you!"

"Cue is joining me in my business. He's officially the Logistics Manager of Texas Tea, LLC. We actually had our first full day today and it went great!"

"Well ain't that something. Congratulations Cue! Now, sit yourselves down and let's fix both of you a plate and celebrate your first official day!"

Tater and Cueball took a table by the window. Cueball, out of habit, slid the Heinz ketchup bottle close to his side of the red checkered covered table top. Tater leaned over and took in the fragrance of the small vase of flowers that had been picked fresh from the field next door. The room was filled with the warmth of Sallie Jean and the aroma of fresh baked cherry pie. Cueball had a mind to skip dinner altogether and head straight for the dessert case, but the growl in his stomach told him otherwise.

"What's the special tonight Sallie Jean?"

"Well, we've got a couple. Got a good mess of catfish caught down by the Lake Livingston Dam Marina this mornin'. We fry that up and add some fresh cut french fries and a handful of jalapeño cheese hush puppies and coleslaw. Or, you can always settle into that giant sized lightly breaded chicken fried steak slathered in homemade cream gravy with a huge scoop of homemade mashed taters."

"Good Lord, I'll take the catfish," proclaimed Tater.

"I'll take the chicken fried steak. Can I have extra gravy on the side please? And, does that come with Texas Toast?"

"Sure does, Cue, and a house salad as well. Coming right up!"

Sallie Jean skipped off into the kitchen leaving Tater and Cueball to conversation. Tater looked at Cueball and gave him a wink. Cueball looked at Tater, then looked behind him, then looked at Tater again.

"What?"

"You kinda sweet on her ain't ya? You always have been Cue, ever since kindergarten."

Cueball's face and bald head turned redder than the McIlhenny's Tabasco bottle that sat on the table. Tater laughed out loud.

"Cue, we are definitely going to need more equipment in at least six months. I'm so glad Daddy bought ten acres to allow for expansion."

"I know what I'm going to do with the money you're payin' me Tater."

"What's that Cue?"

"The first thing I'm gonna do is save for a new truck. That Nova has certainly seen its better days. I'll always be thankful to Coon-Ass Joe for handing it down to me. Then, I'm going to find a place nearby to call my own. I can't thank you enough, Tater, for the chance you're takin' on me. I promise to do you right!"

As they took their last bites and gulped down the last swaller of sweet tea, Sallie Jean came around and plopped two plates of cherry pie on the table and said, "Dessert's on the house as in recognition of the new business and your first day of operations!"

Tater jumped up and gave her a big hug. Cueball jumped up reflexively and hugged Sallie Jean too. He stopped immediately, threw his hands by his side, extended one hand out to her taking her hand and shaking it. Tater could barely contain the amusement she had just witnessed. Sallie Jean started fanning herself. Tater plopped money and a tip on the table and said, "Gotta go, can we take these to go please?"

THE EVICTION

After dinner, Tater dropped Cueball off to pick up his car. Tired, full and happy about the day, he headed back to his trailer behind Ouida's icehouse. Ouida's icehouse was basically a no-frills juke joint, beer shack, place to get snookered without much fuss. As he stepped up to his trailer, Ouida met him at the door.

"Well, how the hell was your first damn day at the tea house? Did you think you needed to wake every motherfucker up on the river bottom leaving so goddamn early this mornin'? When are you goin' to be able to get to those jobs I had for you to do, done around here? I've got so much shit that needs to get done and I'm counting on you to hold up to your end of our agreement. We need to tar the bar roof, remove that goddamn poison ivy off the chain link fence over there and help fence the outdoor patio area by Saturday night! You know you don't live here for free! We had a fuckin' arrangement and I'm afraid you are not going to keep your end of the bargain with the shitty assed high-falutin' job you have Mr. Cue!"

Cueball had just been ambushed by hurricane Ouida and was stumped for words to respond.

"I'll get to them after work tomorrow and the remainder of the week. They will all be done come Saturday afternoon."

"You better as hell believe they will get done Cue! I'm expecting it!"

Cueball stomped into his trailer, slammed the door, dressed for bed and was out like a light. He was startled by his alarm the next morning. This time he got dressed and stepped outside only to find Ouida waiting for him.

"That goddamn alarm woke me up again this fuckin' mornin'! Who the hell do you think you are, you piece of livin' shit! I can't take all this noise in the mornin'! I need my fuckin' beauty sleep on account of the late hours I spend runnin' the icehouse! I've decided that I don't want you on my property any longer. Now get your shit and leave!"

Cueball was shocked by the sudden onslaught of Ouida that morning. He stepped back into the trailer and emerged with a stuffed duffel bag and a couple of paper grocery sacks filled with his meager belongings. He tossed them into his car, turned to Ouida, shot her the middle finger, spat on the ground. He hopped into his Nova and barreled out of the parking lot.

Tater heard Cueball stop in the parking lot but it was another fifteen minutes until she realized he hadn't come into the office. She stepped out the front door and found Cueball still in his car with his face in his hands.

"Cue! What's wrong?"

"That motherfuckin' Ouida Mae kicked me out of my place

this morning all on account that she expects me to do all this work for her while I'm workin' for you! To top it all off, I just think she is jealous that I'm in your good graces again and you have given me the damn chance of a lifetime. Fuck her!"

"Yeah, fuck her! You don't worry about a thing. We will work things out. Now, get out of that car, I've got something to show you."

Cueball got out of the car and followed Tater over to the garage. She threw open the door and behind it was another red Dodge Ram Hemi Dually Diesel with Texas Tea, LLC plastered all over it.

"What ya need another truck for Tater?"

"Dumbass, this one is for the new Logistics Manager! I can't have him driving around town in a no good broken down Nova!"

Cueball fell flat on his ass and started crying.

"I can't believe you are being so damn good to me Tater Murphy! What did I ever do to deserve this?"

"Well, you know there is one condition for you driving this truck besides never getting behind the wheel drunk?"

"What's that?"

"You have to keep working here! For the rest of your life my friend!"

"You can count on that Tater Murphy!"

"And, as for your living arrangements, Daddy has a trailer

on one of our lots and I think he will be just fine with you staying there. He will, of course, ask for a bit of rent and you pay the utilities every month. You good with that?"

Cueball nodded his head and started crying again.

Tater went into her office, picked up the phone and called her daddy.

"Hi Daddy!"

"Well, mornin' Light of my Life! How is my darling daughter today?"

"Daddy, I have a huge favor to ask you. You know that trailer you have on the lot down Jesse Ln? Cue is in a bind on account Ouida kicked him off her property this morning and he needs a new place to live. I told him that you would require rent every month and have to pay utilities as well. He said he would be fine with that. Are you OK with that idea?"

"Well, do I have a choice now that you have promised it to him? Of course I don't mind. Nice thing about that spot is it sits right next to Mr. Lobo and Mrs. Carol's place. They will keep a good eye on him to make sure he doesn't get into any trouble. They're my party line to that area of the river bottom."

"I love you Daddy! I'll give Cue the good news. Talk to you later."

"I love you my Tater."

Tater hung up the phone and shared the good news with Cueball. Because they didn't have a sludge truck coming in until early afternoon, they headed down the road to the property to drop Cueball's things off and introduce him to Mr. Lobo and Mrs. Carol.

As Tater and Cueball turned the corner at Jesse Ln and FM 1127, she could see Mr. Lobo and Mrs. Carol sitting out on their back porch. She tooted her horn and waved. Mr. Lobo stood up and waved smiling back at them. They drove up to Cueball's new digs. The property was about a quarter acre with a gently used single wide trailer on it. The trailer was set up on blocks like most in the area and had air conditioning window units hanging from the most strategic locations in the house. There was a deck built off the front entrance and a smaller porch built off the back. On each side of the trailer were two huge old pecan trees that literally must have been there since creation. A rooster crowed in the distance and from the direction the sound came Tater determined it must be Mr. Lobo's rooster Fandango. Tater punched in a code on the lockbox attached to the water meter, removed the keys and handed them to Cueball. Cueball hopped up on the front deck, slid the key into the lock and popped open the front door. A musty smell hit him square in the face which caused he and Tater to promptly open all the windows in the house to air it out. Other than that, the trailer was actually near Taj Mahal quality for the river bottom. No holes in the floor, decent mini blinds on the windows, a refrigerator, stove, microwave and added bonus. . .a washer and dryer. The trailer was moderately furnished as well with a bed and dresser in both bedrooms, a Mid-Century sofa and La-Z-Boy recliner in the living room. Cueball had never lived in such a nice place before and was glad to have the space. He took his belongings to the back bedroom and emptied them into the dresser.

"Come on Cue, let me introduce you to Mr. Lobo and Mrs. Carol before we head back to the office."

Tater and Cueball walked next door to Mr. Lobo and Mrs. Carol's property. The gate entrance was always open during the day when Mr. Lobo was home so Tater and Cueball walked right through. Their property was about an acre. Smack dab in the middle of the lot rested their house which had originally been a single wide trailer. Mr. Lobo had taken it upon himself, when he first moved the trailer to the lot, to expand the structure making it twice the size a house it started out to be. Once the outer walls were built, he tore down the inner walls just about removing all signs of the mobile home in its former glory. He also built a huge wrap around porch and instead of railings, he and Mrs. Carol adorned it with driftwood they had picked up on their many fishing trips. It was absolutely beautiful. Most passerby's mistook it for a custom log cabin. On one side of the house was about a quarter acre of garden that he and Mrs. Carol tended to every year. You could see the nice juicy red tomatoes from the road. They also grew pole beans, okra, corn, jalapeños, serranos,

Ichiban eggplant and squash amongst other things. It was amazing how much food they had in that small little area. Mrs. Carol had a reputation as the best canner in the county on account of the fantastic canning room Mr. Lobo had built for her. It was complete with shelves, stove top and sink so she could put all their harvest away at the end of growing season each year. Behind the garden was a chicken coop full of Bantam hens and a majestic white, black and gray Leghorn rooster named Fandango.

Out of nowhere came this huge "Hoooooooonkkk!" Tater and Cueball near jumped out of their shoes. By that time Mr. Lobo had appeared on the front porch and laughed out loud at the sight.

"That's Matilda, she's our watch goose."

"She shore is a beautiful goose, sir," proclaimed Cueball.

"Did you just get more handsome or just slightly taller Mr. Lobo?"

"Still about six feet and rugged as ever, Tater."

Mr. Lobo tucked his red hair under the sweat stained Stowaway Marina ball cap that adorned his head. He scratched his multi-colored beard hugging his face as he winked at them.

"Watch this!" grinned Mr. Lobo.

He stood up on his tippy toes and started flapping his arms beside him like he was going to fly and yelled, "Think Pretty Matilda!"

Almost immediately that beautiful white goose stood up on her feet and began waving her wings and honking back at him. Tater and Cueball looked at each other in amazement.

"That's a wonderful goose you have there Mr. Lobo. I bet it took a long time to teach her that."

"Nope, not long at all. Who's that you got there with you Tater Bell?"

Mr. Lobo had a nickname for everyone he called friend or family and Tater appreciated the sentiment.

"This is Johnny 'Cueball' Whitehead."

"Hi Mr. Lobo," responded Cueball.

"Well, hello there padna! Looks like you are going to be me and Mrs. Carol's new neighbor."

"Yessir."

"He's my new Logistics Manager at the shop also."

"Well, ain't that something! Congratulations Cue! I've heard your name around town and am happy to meet you. You are welcome to drop by any time. Mrs. Carol and I spend our evenings breathing the fresh country air on the back porch, wetting our whistles with an adult beverage or two. Our door is always open to a friend of Tater's."

"Thank you sir. I will definitely take you up on the invite. It will be great living next to nice folk like you."

About that time Tater let out a yelp.

"Samson! Stop sniffing my butt you sweet boy! This here's

Samson, Mr. Lobo's Shepherd watch dog. If he don't know you, he'll eat you alive. If you don't show no harm, he'll be your best friend."

Mrs. Carol stepped outside and exclaimed, "You aren't inflating Lobo's head or anything like that now Tater are you?"

Everyone laughed and Mr. Lobo introduced her to Cueball.

"Would you yunguns like to come in for a glass of tea?"

"Thank you, Mrs. Carol, but Cue and I need to get back to the shop. We're expecting a delivery. We will drop by when we have more time."

Tater and Cueball waved goodbye and headed back to their vehicle driving off to the office.

Backup Plan

Tater spent the next couple of months building her business. She felt comfortable with Cueball running the shop when she had to get on the road to drum up more customers. Within that time she visited just about every corner of Texas, Oklahoma and Louisiana. Everyone she met was left with some sort of Texas Tea, LLC paraphernalia. She scheduled her sludge deliveries by areas of state on each day. For instance, Mondays were East Texas days, Tuesdays were Bayou days, Wednesdays were Sooner days, Thursdays and Fridays were West Texas and Central Texas days respectively. Cueball had four sludge trucks coming in each morning and was sending out a tanker every afternoon. Tater landed a couple of very large contracts with oil changing chains in Texas, Oklahoma and Louisiana. She would begin taking their deliveries and sending out the recycled materials the weeks following. This nearly doubled business for Tater and Texas Tea, LLC. Next steps for her would be to lay out plans for future expansion of the facility. The investors were extremely happy with the progress Tater had made in such a short time. They were equally as amazed at her ability to stick her neck into this good ole boy world and begin blazing a trail for herself. Capacity had maxed out. It was time for Tater to get the second processor going and had a third on its way. Needless to say, August was going to be a very busy month for them.

Cueball had been doing very well since he left Ouida's property. In fact, he didn't give her much of a thought on account he was so busy at Texas Tea. He was working twelve hour days, six days a week. Five days were spent servicing the vehicles and the sixth was used to clean up the shop and yard to get ready for the next week. He didn't have time to get into trouble and was happy for it. The operation had become so busy that Tater asked him to hire another person to help with the menial tasks. She wanted him to understand how to operate the servers in the office that tied to the equipment in the yard. Although he wasn't a techie sort of fella, she told him it was very easy and if he ever had any problems he could call their tech guy over in the Woodlands who could assist via the phone or would come into town to help out if need be. Tater asked Marvin Marks, their computer genius, to come to town for a week to ensure Cueball had all the training he needed to understand that part of the operation. Marvin spent the week showing Cueball the ins and outs of the servers and main computer so that by the time Marvin headed out, Cueball felt confident he could run things on this end. Tater couldn't have been happier with the progress.

Cueball hired another gal by the name of Patty Dunstan to help out at the shop. Patty arrived at the shop about a month in to Cueball's employment.

"Cue, I can't thank you enough for the opportunity."

"Well, Patty, we need to get you into more presentable attire other than those Walmart pajama jeans and slip on tenny shoes."

Patty looked down at her KISS t-shirt and back up at Cueball as if she didn't understand what he exactly meant by that comment.

"I just hope we have something that fits your skinny self," said Cueball.

Patty stood there twirling her bleached blonde hair accented with a pukey green shimmer that only a bad batch of bleach could muster up. Cueball handed her a couple of hangers adorned with the company uniform. Patty didn't mind a new pair of duds.

Patty had a work ethic that would run circles around just about anyone in town. She didn't mind rolling up her sleeves and digging into the grit and grime of the operations. She had a personality as big as life and although she wasn't the purtiest thing you laid your eyes on, the drivers loved her. Patty's vernacular was that of a trucker's and she was tough as nails. She wouldn't take shit off of anyone. She drove an old Chevy 1500 that she purchased off Mrs. Carol a while back since Mrs. Carol wasn't able to drive any longer. She had a pit bull mix by the name of Daisy who followed her everywhere she went.

Tater stepped out on the porch.

"Patty, I'm so glad Cue coerced you into working with us."

"Thanks Tater, I appreciate the opportunity."

Tater took in the activity in the work yard that morning and felt confident she had a great crew which could only mean three things. . .stability, progress and growth.

"Beep Beep Be Beep Beep Beep Beep," honked Murphy as he pulled into the yard.

"Hey there Mr. Murphy!" greeted Patty.

"Well, hey there Patty darlin'. Tater told me you joined the company and it's good seeing you again!"

"Thank you sir."

"Tater, that container with the new processing equipment is on its way. We should have it here on the lot by Friday afternoon. I would suppose you already have a spot for it cleared away? Just want to make sure you're prepared for the delivery. Also, will Marvin be here next Monday to connect it to the mainframe?"

"Now Daddy, you seriously didn't think I haven't thought about all that? Cue and Patty have spent the last couple of afternoons clearing the area and we are going to place that in section three over there,"

Tater pointed over to the east end of the yard.

"We are good to go Daddy and don't you worry. Marvin is ready and will be here at eight sharp come Monday morning."

About that time Daisy came running up on the porch and jumped up on Murphy nearly knocking him off his feet.

Patty laughed and blurted out, "Wow! Daisy ain't never took to no one like that first off before. She shore does like you Mr. M!"

Murphy gave Daisy a good back rub, pulled a dog bone out of his pocket and stuck it in her mouth. Daisy ran off happily. Murphy brushed his jeans off, tipped his hat, and gave Tater a peck on the cheek.

"I'll see you all on Monday then. Love you Tater, good seeing you Cue and Patty. Oh, by the way, ya'll goin' to the square dance in a few weeks?"

"Square dance? When the heck have we ever had a square dance here in the river bottom?" asked Cueball.

"The quilting ladies are in their annual fundraiser mode and thought this would be a good idea to get the town together and support their efforts in making quilts for our service men and women," answered Patty.

"Well, then, this will be a great opportunity to share a little Texas Tea love and give to a good cause. I say we all go!" exclaimed Tater.

With that Murphy hopped into his truck and headed off.

"Mr. M really does trust you're going to do right by him with this here business Tater. Good for you!" Patty proclaimed.

Marvin arrived at the office on Monday as planned. He claimed to be a self-taught techie who learned the basics in high school. He worked for various companies in The Woodlands, Texas honing his trade and then went into business for himself. His passion focused on connecting small businesses with the latest technology available to make the work experience highly user friendly.

"Hey, Marvin. Glad you could make it today. How long do you think it will take you to set up the new equipment?"

"Well, Tater, since I'm walking Cueball through the process and writing up standard operating procedures for reference, it might take until Wednesday. We shall see."

About that time the front door of the headquarters swung open and Cueball appeared. "Hey Cue, ready to get to work?"

"Darn right Marvin! Is that your nerd uniform? I heard Hilfiger polos were part of the dress code of nerds."

"Funny Cue, now let's get serious."

Marvin scratched the scruff of his beard and stuck a Dum Dum sucker in his mouth. He motioned for Cueball to follow him to the server room. The new equipment had arrived as planned the Friday before and Marvin was ready to run the cables and set up the servers that were used for the processors. Processor #2 was set up to handle the expansion of the business. Processor #3 was set up and standing by as a backup to the other processors if one of them failed, or when business grew over the next few months.

Tater went outside to survey the work underway about the same time Murphy drove up.

"Tater, how are you doing this fine morning my darling daughter?"

"Doing great now that you're here Daddy!"

"Well, I have a surprise for you my dear. Now that you are installing the additional processors and can barely handle the output from the one you have now, I've decided to give you two more tankers to haul your profit off!"

About that time an army of workers arrived.

"On what side do you want to extend the parking lot?"

Tater looked at her daddy dumbfounded and pointed to the east end of the property near where the new processing unit was being installed.

"Guys, let's go lay us a slab for the new trucks!"

They all proceeded over to the east end of the lot and began digging and laying rebar for the new parking area. Tater couldn't believe her eyes but was delighted all the same that her daddy would go out of his way to do something like this for her.

"Daddy, you are amazing! What can I do to ever thank you enough?"

"Just keep growing this business and make that amazing name for yourself my dear."

It took the crew three days to get the lot prepped and

poured for the new trucks. It took Marvin and Cueball the same amount of time to wrap up the mechanical and technical aspects of the work.

Patty set up a training session in the main meeting room of the office and two new drivers and a yard guy were in attendance. She went over the company manual with them and gave them the spiel of ethics in the workplace and how Tater believed in treating her team with dignity and respect expecting the same in return from each of them. She stressed the importance of being on time, wearing a clean company uniform and the extra added benefit of breakfast being served each morning as an incentive to get them to show up at work promptly to kick off each day.

Friday afternoon brought a little cool front into town. The very thing that makes us locals want to sit around and shoot the breeze rather than dig in and get any work done. This was apparent at Texas Tea. Tater, Cueball, Patty and Marvin had settled onto the porch for a break when what sounded like a honking parade headed down FM1127 towards Texas Tea. They jumped to their feet when they realized what was going on. Two new tankers were turning the corner emblazoned with the familiar Texas Tea, LLC logo on each side. Patty rushed into the yard and directed the tankers to the new parking area that had been laid near Processors 2 and 3.

"This is becoming a big time operation Tater!"

"Sure is Cue, I can't be more happy."

"Pretty soon, you're gunna have to expand onto that extry land you purchased. I sure hope you don't run out of space Tater!"

"Not counting on that, Cue. Your concern does not go unnoticed. Shows me you are thinking like a real business man."

Cueball's face blushed pink as a winter sunset.

Mr. Lobo settled into his home office and picked up the hammer on his CB radio base station.

"Breaker, breaker, Veggie Man."

"Copy that Papa Bear."

"Just followed a parade of Texas Tea eighteen wheelers on my way home from McMann's."

"10-4 Papa Bear. I saw them fly by the vegetable stand about an hour ago. Looks like Tater's taking delivery on a few new shiny ones."

"Copy that Veggie Man. That Tater and Old Man Murphy have set them up quite an operation."

"10-4 Papa Bear. It's definitely the talk of the town these days. There's buzz all over town on how Tater is going to expand that business all over the good ole U S of A."

"Well, I don't know if I would go that far Veggie Man. However, I'm sure glad that sweet gal has a great business going for her. Momma is real proud that a little lady has been able to make a name for herself for once in this here river bottom."

About that time Mrs. Carol appeared in the doorway.

"Lobo, what are you gabbing about now? Tell Sam I said hello."

"Hello there Mamma Bear! I can smell your good cooking all the way up here on the main highway."

"Oh Sam, I bet you say that to all the gals."

Mr. Lobo winked at Mrs. Carol.

"Momma, I was telling Sam about the tankers rolling down FM 1147 on my way home. I should take you over to Tater's and give you a tour."

Mrs. Carol smiled and turned to head back into the kitchen. Mr. Lobo gave her a love pat on the backside prompting her to swing around and throw her finger up in his face.

"Lobo, you keep those dirty hands off of me or I'll go get my skillet."

She headed down the hall laughing as she went.

"She told you Papa Bear."

"She always does Veggie Man. Gotta go. Over and out."

"Over and Out."

The next morning Dwanna's phone rang in her pocket. She was over at the Tabernacle in the middle of her weekly prayer meeting when one of the prickly old sisters in the group glared her a self righteous glare. Dwanna slapped her pocket, got up and headed into the hallway outside the sanctuary.

"Hello, this is Dwanna, how may I help you?"

"Dwanna, did you hear about that caravan of trucks headed to Tater's shop yesterday?"

"Well, precious one, I sure did."

"I saw them drive in front of my icehouse and head down FM 1127. There were hundreds of them. Held up traffic for hours."

"For hours? You don't say."

"What, you think I'm fuckin' lyin' or sumthin'? I kid you not Dwanna. The inconvenience of it all and yet no one seemed to give a lick about all the goins on."

"Well, surely it's a good sign when Tater takes delivery of new vehicles. Must mean she is doing well. The Lord is definitely blessing her little sweet heart."

"Goddamnit, Dwanna. Why in the mutherfuckin' hell do you have to bring Jesus H Christ into every sorry ass conversation we have?"

"Now, Ouida."

"I'll tell you one thing Dwanna. That fuckin' traffic jam did one good thing for my business. Apparently everyone was so interested in what was happenin' they decided to come set a spell and watch the spectacle from my icehouse. We sold more beer yesterday than we do on any typical Friday. It was a drop dead early morning happy hour that I haven't seen in quite a while."

"Well, the Lord does work in miraculous ways."

"There you go again Dwanna."

"What are you doing for Thanksgiving Ouida?"

"I'll be opening the icehouse at the same time. I have catered a few smoked turkeys from Momma Floyd's at the Lunch Shack over on Lilly Hill."

"She does a great smoked turkey doesn't she Ouida?"

"Yes, she sure does and she is throwin' in all the fixins. Drop by if you can Dwanna. Would love to see you."

"Remind me of the Legend of Lilly Hill, Ouida."

"Well, Dwanna, story has it that FM 1127 was a cotton and ranching community way back in the day. Many of the landowners had sharecroppers living on their property. Those sharecroppers were actually slaves. After the end of slavery, the landowners gave parcels of their land to their freed slaves as a recompense for their wrongs. The new owners handed down their land to their families for generations. Momma Floyd, as she was affectionately known, was one of those such descendants. She owns ten acres of land. On the land is a pecan orchard and a field of lilies that when they bloomed you would have thought snow had fallen. That's where she opened her little shack on the roadside where she offers soul food lunches to those in the area. Nothing fancy but the best tasting collards, oxtails and fried chicken this side of anywhere.

Momma Floyd was a legend in the area. Some folk say she

got into a situation with her former husband. He had been coming home drunk every night and beating her black and blue for years. One evening, Momma Floyd had had enough and gagged him, then tied him up. She cut his fingers and toes off one by one with her pruning shears. She then dragged him out into the dark of the night, over to Old Man Pinkie's swamp and offered him up as a snack to the fourteen foot alligator folks know as Jethro in this here neck of the woods. That's the story anyway. You wouldn't think a sweet little woman like that could do such a horrid thing. Regardless, it's a legend as there was no evidence to be found. Her old man just up and disappeared one day."

Square Dance

Preparations for the square dance paid off this warm September evening. Tater met Patty and Cueball at the community center across from the elementary school. There were cars, trucks and motorcycles from all over San Jacinto and Polk County parked out front. There were even a couple of big rigs parked on the main road. High school kids were hanging out behind the building smoking stogies thinking no one else could see them. Other kids were playing basketball on the court next to the center. Tater pulled into the parking lot. She had no mind to change out of her workwear so as she could get her company name out to more folks who hadn't heard about it yet. Right about that time Cueball and Patty drove up in their vehicles. Cueball and Patty both had the same idea as Tater and had put on a fresh uniform for the dance. They all exited their vehicles about the same time. Patty spoke up.

"We all look like walking billboard Tater."

"We sure do Patty!"

They headed into the community center together greeted by the sound of a local band playing a great set of bluegrass to get the mood going for the dance. Over to the left of the room was a fifteen foot long dessert table and over it hung a big banner that read "First Annual Quilting Bee Military Support Square Dance". The table was covered in a burlap tablecloth strewn with meringue pies, fruit pies, cobblers, brownies, cupcakes, layer cakes, basically anything that would meet your sweet tooth fancy. At the end was a huge glass punch bowl filled with limeade, ginger ale and a sherbet floater. A donation box was set next to it. Tater had written a company check for $1,000.00 and stuck it in the box. She looked back at Cueball and Patty.

"This is from us."

Cueball and Patty both smiled and gave a thumbs up.

The room began filling up with more locals when Sallie Jean walked up and gave Cueball a big hug. Cueball blushed and Tater and Patty's winked at him simultaneously.

"Hi Cue, how you doin'?" asked Sallie Jean as she beamed from ear to ear.

She nervously twisted her hips from side to side fanning out her pretty little pink and chartreuse green ruffled square dance skirt as she rocked back and forth on her black patent leather dancing heels adorned with frilly ankle socks.

"Doin' fine Sallie Jean."

Sallie Jean turned to Tater and Patty.

"I've got some cherry pie and chocolate meringue on the dessert table. Mine's the ones on the plates with strawberries and butterflies. Hope you have some!"

Sallie Jean extended her hand to Cueball.

"How would you like to dance the first dance with me tonight?"

"Sure, Sallie Jean, if you can stand my two left feet."

"Grab your padna do-si-do, let's kick this off with a big fat show!" came an announcement from the square dance caller.

The band struck up the melody and the dancing crowd went electric. Sallie Jean grabbed Cueball's hand and pulled him out on the dance floor.

"Chicken in the bread pan, scratching out gravel, get your maid and away you travel," continued the caller.

Cueball looked like a deer in headlights as he was whirled away by Sallie Jean. Tater and Patty were enjoying the night already.

On the other side of the dance floor Dwanna was working the crowd ensuring that everyone was having a good time. She reached to the end of the sleeve of her western shirt adorned with roses and pearl snaps pressing one of the snaps back together.

"I see you traded those hiking boots in for dancing shoes tonite Dwanna," said Tater.

"Tater Murphy, you know it. I'm so glad you made it tonite!"

"Well, I'm happy to be here. I'm headed towards that cherry pie and will catch ya later Dwanna."

As folks approached Dwanna's side of the hall she would

give them a "Jesus is blessing you for being here tonight. Don't forget the donation box at the end of the buffet!" greeting. She set up a display of quilts all over the hall for everyone to see and a silent auction slip was pinned to each of them with a minimum bid of $250. Folks were already kicking off the bids on the quilts and Dwanna was tickled pink.

"Damnit Dwanna!" came a voice from behind her.

Dwanna turned around and found Ouida standing right in front of her.

"I thought you weren't coming!"

"Well, I decided it was good for business if I showed up tonight. Besides, you did say there was going to be some good looking eligible men here."

"Ouida, you sure do look pretty in that flowered sundress and strappy sandals."

Ouida blushed as she fluffed her teased coif around her ears.

"You look like a model out of a 50s fashion magazine, precious one."

Ouida wasn't sure whether she should take that as a compliment or not.

"Shut up! I just thought it was important to represent appropriately at this here square dance tonight."

"Hand over hand, heel over heel, the faster you go, the better you feel," continued the caller.

Ouida then pointed to Cueball on the dance floor with Sallie Jean.

"Imagine that. That mutherfucker Cue got him a girlfriend in Sallie Jean from the diner! He's such a piece of shit. He walks around town like he's better than everybody with his new job at Tater's shop. He seems to have fuckin' forgot that I taught him ever-thang he knows. He left my property with no good bye, no fuck you, no nothing! Sorry ass sonofabitch!"

Dwanna glared at Ouida. Her face quickly softened with empathy to show Ouida she cared about her misfortune.

"Honor your corner and your partner too, wave at the gal across from you," crowed the caller.

Cueball looked up and waved the middle finger of fellowship directly at Ouida. Ouida turned around, bent over and threw her skirt up mooning Cueball in response. Dwanna jerked Ouida's skirt down and slapped her on the ass in disgust.

"Some girls are pretty, some are not, but boy you're stuck with the one you've got," continued the caller.

The band was full-blown amplification by now and the room was charged with playful energy. Not a person present was sitting down and whether they were dancing or not, everyone's feet were a tappin'.

Suddenly a hand grabbed Patty's and drug her out on the dance floor. Cherokee Johnson, an electrician from town, was her regular guy. He was a biker through and through. Although a bad accident a year or so ago took him off his Indian forever, he still looked the look and talked the talk.

Patty reached over and grabbed his scraggly ZZ Top beard and kissed him square on the lips.

"I'm so glad you went out of your way to wear your dirty old work boots. I can see my reflection in those worn out steel-toes. Perhaps we go into Livingston tomorrow and pick you up a new pair?"

"You think so, you old hussy?"

"Shut up and dance you hunk of burnin love."

Cherokee pulled Patty up against his Stevie Nicks t-shirt covered beer belly and swung her around the room.

"The good girls walk, the bad girls ride, come on bad girl, my cars outside," the caller continued.

"Damn Cherokee, you smell like a sour mashaholic."

"Just a lil home grown moonshine," proclaimed Cherokee.

Cherokee danced Patty right out the front door never to return to the dance that night. Mr. Murphy passed Cherokee and Patty on the way in.

"Good night you lovebirds!"

Cherokee and Patty waved goodbye to Murphy.

Murphy entered the dance hall as music flowed through the air reminding him of his high school days. The smell of chocolate cake led him directly to the dessert table where he immediately took care of his sweet tooth. Tater walked up to him.

“Daddy, it’s [illegible] e had so much fun so far and the [illegible]

About that time Cueball and Sallie Jean stepped off the dance floor and greeted Murphy. They were bent over out of breath and giggly over the dance they just wrapped up. Cueball actually had his arm around Sallie Jean.

“Hi Mr. Murphy,” approached Dwanna, “I saw you come in and was so glad to see you could make it! We’ve got all kinds of quilts up for auction tonight and there’s a donation box at the end of the dessert table if you feel led to give to our cause this evening. By the way, when are we going to see you at the Tabernacle? We would love to have you join us one Sunday for service or Wednesday evening for Bible study.”

Murphy smiled at Dwanna then looked over at Tater and gave her the “Don’t say a word look”. Tater grabbed her daddy, rescuing him, and pulled him out on the dance floor.

“Up the river and around the bend, all hold hands we’re off again!” proclaimed the caller. “Bow to your partner, and the corner miss, to the opposite lady, just blow a kiss.”

Murphy blew a kiss too fast to realize it was going straight over to Ouida. Tater caught what had just happened and nearly peed her pants.

“She’s a real looker huh Daddy.”

Murphy looked at Tater and made a gagging sound as they

continued on around the dance floor.

"Pick out a quilt, throw a dollar in, let's make this night a big fat win!" exclaimed the caller.

Tater and her daddy swung around the dance floor for the next two dances until they couldn't take it any longer. They returned to the dessert table to get a cup of punch when Ouida made her way around to Tater.

"Evenin' Taaaaater. How's your erl biness doin' these days? I hope Cue is workin' hard fer ya cuz he didn't do shit for me. In fact, he abandoned me as soon as you gave him that job. Would you mind letting him know there are still some things around the icehouse that need his attention? He still has some chores to wrap up over there."

"What's between you and Cue stays between you and Cue, Ouida Mae. I'm not getting in the middle of that, Ouida, and you can stay out of my business as well!"

Ouida swung around and stomped off towards the other side of the room. Murphy looked at Tater and said, "That's my girl!"

"Chicken in the bread pan, pickin' out dough, big pig rootin' up the little tater now," continued the caller.

Tater and her daddy returned to the floor to go another round.

The night continued on with music, dance, donations and no sign of scuffle. Everyone came with the intent to give to the community and enjoy the fun as a unified town. Cameras were snappin' all over the place to capture the events of the evening. Love was in the air for a few and possibly some little ones were conceived that night as a result. Can't say there was another night as free and fun filled with energy as that evening was. Someone even spiked the punch by the end of the evening. Dwanna was aghast after finding a couple of empty ball jars under the dessert table reeking of alcohol. Folks will have stories to tell for generations about the square dance. To top it off, the quilting bee raised $10,000 dollars from individuals as well as companies to support the fundraising efforts for the troops. Dwanna couldn't have been happier.

Ouida's Icehouse

Ouida opens her icehouse every day at seven in the morning like all faithful rum runners do. The icehouse is nothing more than a long white tin shack with garage doors lining the highway side of the road. You could probably park two big rigs end to end in it if you tried. Inside you would find the typical motif of neon beer signs adorned with scantily clad ladies, a couple of coin-op pool tables, a one-armed bandit, a trivia machine, a dance floor for when she had a band come play, and of course the bar. The place stunk to high heaven from years of stale spilled beer complemented by cigarette smoke that had stained everything in the bar. She had room outside for a barbecue pit and wooden picnic tables in the event someone would rather sit outside than in. She would throw those garage doors up and flip the Miller High Life sign on as a signal to the community of her being open for business. Her security system was a Remington, double barrel sawed off shotgun under the bar as well as a Colt .38 special tucked in her pocket. Ouida wasn't afraid of anyone or anything and felt she was protected well enough in that place.

Her barmaid Deirdre was working there to make her way through cosmetology school. She always looked like a train wreck when she got in each morning. Between school and her late night partying she was well worn out before the day even began.

"Hey Deirdre, looks like you had quite a night."

Deirdre adjusted the belt of her secondhand Lucky Brand Jeans, rubbed her two day old mascara covered bloodshot eyes and said, "You got that right Ouida. Can't say I got much sleep last night."

Ouida also had a group of regulars who worked the late shift at the local sawmill and would show up right as the welcome mat was rolled out. They considered this time of the morning their happy hour and plunked quite a bit of change on her bar each day.

Coon-Ass Joe, the town drunk, and his dog Gomer were daily patrons of Ouida's establishment. Coon-Ass Joe looked to be about 80 and probably wasn't a day over 60. His body pickled with the liquor he drank from the time he got up until the time he went to bed. His eyes were constantly glazed over and gave one the impression he wasn't quite present in the moment.

"Mornin' Joe, what can I get ya?"

"Hey dar Ouida. Ah 'spose one o dem tallboys to get me started tank ya."

Joe ran his fingers through his white hair slicked back with Brylcreem. He put his thumbs behind the bib of his Dickie's overalls and kicked his pointy toed Tony Lama snakeskin cowboy boots against the bar adjusting himself in his perch. The only jewelry he wore was his wedding ring. He threw his watch away after retirement never to keep an eye on time again. He smelled mighty fine also from that picklin' and most folks didn't sit near him when they came to the bar as a result. They say he lost his wife twenty years ago and ever since then he decided to drink his sorrows away. You would wonder how in the world he could support such a drinking habit. One reason was because Ouida felt bad for the guy on account his wife treated her like the daughter she never had and therefore let Joe drink free after four each day. Secondly, he had a bit of a fortune tucked away due to the life insurance policy he had out on his wife which kept his habit going strong.

Gomer was Coon-Ass Joe's dog. A junkyard dog that he rescued from out front of the bar a few years ago. Gomer was a mangy-ass lookin' thing and meaner than shit. Folks say he lost his back left foot when he was out snoopin' around the cedar swamp off Old Man Pinkie's property when a gator lunged out of the water at him. He was missing his right eye on account he tangled up with a raccoon one summer day fighting over a nice fresh batch of road kill. He also had a big chunk of flesh missing out of his right side from getting hit by a four wheeler driven by some stupid ass kids in town. The most fragrant thing about him was he always smelled as though he had been dancin' with a pole cat. Believe it or not, Gomer also had a vice. He loved the taste of whisky. Not any whisky in particular, just whatever he could get that nasty ass dog tongue on. Coon-Ass Joe and Ouida supported his addiction also. He could always count on one of them giving him a shot of whisky when he came into the bar with Coon-Ass Joe. Not sure if that was to stay in his good graces or to simply keep him calm so he didn't do any of the customers harm.

Dwanna dropped by the icehouse on that crisp October morning to take Ouida a fresh baked pan of pull-apart jalapeño cheese bread. As she stepped into the icehouse the stench of stale beer and cigarettes hit her square in the nose. Made her nauseated and definitely motivated her not to stay long.

"Are you ever able to get that stinky alcohol smell out of here?"

"Nope, it's part of the ambiance around here and I've gotten pretty used to it by now."

"Well, I brought you some of your favorite bread as I was going to be in the area this morning. Did you know we were able to raise enough money at the square dance to quilt forty blankets and send them off to our troops? You wouldn't believe how much it costs to mail them! It's almost half of what we raised! You would think the boys up in Washington would figure a way to make all this postage to the troops free! But no! I reckon it's yet another way for them to boost the economy. Send them to war, make money. Make more weapons, make money. Kill the enemies, gain control, make more money. Increase mail going out internationally on account of our boys and girls being at war, make more money. Sounds like a darn MasterCard commercial."

Coon-Ass Joe burped, looked up at Dwanna, and exclaimed, "Damn straight! Govment gonna get ya whar de can til dere's nutin' left!" He promptly laid his head back down on the bar for another morning snooze.

"I can see you already liquored up that old dog this morning Ouida."

"Joe's always that way."

"No! I mean that old Gomer. He looks like he's two sheets to the wind."

"Gotta do what ya gotta do to keep the peace around here. By the way, I saw Cue and that Sallie Jean on the dance floor and couldn't believe how damn giddy they looked flitting around the room! I couldn't believe that Sallie Jean would have anything to do with that ugly motherfucker Cue! You know, I'm still angry at Cue! I went straight to Tater to tell her that he still had unfinished business with me and wanted him to get over here and wrap these things up. Do you know what Tater said? She said it wasn't any of her business and she wasn't going to be fuckin' in the middle of things between me and Cue."

"Now honey, you should be happy for Cue. You need to

forgive and move on Ouida!"

Ouida picked up a mason jar and poured herself what appeared to be a glass of water.

"That doesn't smell like water Ouida."

Ouida looked at her and put her forefinger to her mouth as if to say "shhhhh."

"Ouida, where on earth did you get that?"

"I have a friend of a friend who just started sending me this special water so I can distribute it to my close friends here in San Jacinto County and make a little extra money on the side. There's nothing wrong with making a little extra money if no one is the wiser. Don't you go blabbing this off to anyone Dwanna! Otherwise, I'll have your neck!"

"Is it good for you like when you catch cold or somethin'?"

"Damn straight. Here, let me send some home with you free of charge to keep that trap of yours shut."

Ouida pulled a new quart mason jar from under her counter filled three quarters full of moonshine. She wrote on the lid "Rubbing Alcohol" with a Sharpie.

"I won't say a thing Ouida on account this is 'medicine.' How much you makin' on this stuff a week?"

"Well, I suppose I make about five hunnerd dollars after all my write offs."

"Write offs huh? When did you start getting this stuff in?"

"Oh about a week ago from some guy who lives over in

Liberty County. In fact, Dwanna, if you can keep this on the down low and share this with some of your most trusted folks as you send them my way, I'll cut you in on some of that part of the profit. It would definitely help you do some things you been wantin' to do around the house."

"You can count me out of that. I will have nothing to do with this illegal activity that you have decided to take part in Ouida Mae! However, if I hear someone is in need of some medicinal support, I will send them your way free of charge. I'm sure they don't cover this on Obama Care."

Dwanna exited the icehouse and hopped into her car. She turned on the engine and headed her way back into town towards her place. She kept looking at the bottle on the seat next to her thinking, "Lord Jesus, what have I done? Lord, please forgive me! Yes, Lord! I'll get rid of this right now!"

Dwanna slammed on her brakes over in front of Zeke's gas station off US 59, near stumbled out of her vehicle and ran over to the dumpster immediately tossing the mason jar inside. She wiped her hands on her blue jean skirt, hopped back into her car breathing out a sigh of relief as she travelled home. She couldn't believe that Ouida Mae was wrapped up in this mess and really didn't want to have anything to do with it. However, because of her calling, she would keep a close eye on Ouida and make sure she was there to help her when the time came. Perhaps this was a sign from Sweet Jesus that this would be the very opportunity to lead Ouida to Him, through Dwanna, of course.

"Now there is always a silver lining to everything. Thank you Jesus!"

Dwanna drove out of the parking lot and headed back to her house singing "I'll fly away old gloreeeeee".

Local Social

The crisp, coolness of fall had settled in. Signs of Halloween were popping up everywhere. McMann's grocery store was throwing a local apple bobbing contest for the kids to provide parents some relief while they did their grocery shopping. Dwanna was out front with her church sisters peddling their dessert specialties to raise money for the upcoming revival the Tabernacle was putting on.

"Look at those damn holy rollers Patty."

"They mean well Kody. You shouldn't give them such a hard time."

Kody rolled the window of his Toyota Tacoma 4x4 up and cranked the AC on.

"So Patty, when you gonna leave that old man of yours and make it official between you and me?"

"Kody Nash, I don't have any intention of leaving Cherokee. You know that. Besides, you and I are simply friends and business partners."

Kody unscrewed the lid of a ball jar and tossed back the contents.

"You better put that shit down out of sight mister. There's no need to raise suspicion particularly in this here parking lot."

"Ah shit Patty, folks will think I'm just taking a cool sip of water out of this thing."

Patty reached for the door when Kody pulled her back to the center of the seat.

"Where ya goin' so quickly there young lady?"

Patty slapped Kody's hand away and threw him a piercing glare.

"I've got stuff to do today. It's the only day I have to myself and I need to run some errands before it gets away from me."

"Well, just make sure that next delivery is on time. We have a lot of folks counting on you and we wouldn't want to let them down now, would we?"

"No, we sure the shit wouldn't. Besides, I've got bills to pay and Christmas presents to buy so the little bit of extra cash will go a long way with that."

"You ain't gonna set up no retirement plan with that money Patty?"

"Oh hell no, my retirement plan is a can in the dirt thank you very much."

"Ok, now that we have that straight, I'll let you go on about your business. I'll see you at the shop next week."

Patty hopped out of the Toyota and headed into McMann's to pick up some groceries before she headed back to the house.

"Reel it in fast Tater!"

"I'm tryin' my best Daddy but it's a whopper!"

The morning sun was burning off the fog that had settled on the lake. Tater and her daddy were wrestling what seemed to be the biggest bass they ever caught out of Lake Livingston. Murphy had the fish net in one hand and was manning the troll motor to keep Tater in position for bringing the big one in.

"Jesus God, Daddy, he just won't give up the ghost!"

"He sure does appear to be a big one. Give him some slack and then reel him in some more. You will land him sooner than you think Tater!"

Tater continued to fight the creature. Murphy couldn't help but laugh out loud at her trailing up one side of the boat and down the other. He could tell she was getting a bit tired but her determination wasn't going to allow her to give up on this one.

Murphy looked across the lake and thought about the many times he and Tater had spent on every inch of the water seeking out bass, crappie, catfish — hell anything they could catch. He loved the peace and serenity just being on the lake brought to his spirit. This was his church. It was his place to forget about his cares and simply breathe in the beauty that surrounded him.

The line on Tater's fishing pole snapped and Tater when flying backwards landing on the cooler perched in the middle of Murphy's boat.

"Goddamnit! I almost had that fucker!"

Suddenly a fourteen foot log rolled over next to the boat

slamming its tail in the water and swam off.

"Holy Moses Tater! You have been fighting with that old gator all morning!"

"Good God, Daddy! What the hell would we have done had he shown his ugly mug?"

"Well, I would have slammed on the gas and gotten the hell out of here. That's what I would have done. No need to stir up that old man. He's survived this long in the lake, he should be able to stick around for a while Tater."

"Yeah, Daddy, I would agree. No need to become gator bait out here."

Murphy kicked on the motor and headed over to the bridge to see if they would have any luck near the pilings.

"You see that house over there Daddy?"

"That one right off the point?"

"Yes, sir. My friends Ghetto Girl and Lucy Ruth live in that lake house. I'm going to take you over to meet them one day. They both like to fish but that Ghetto Girl is a fanatic. I bet she was out at four this morning dipping her line in just in case."

"That's a pretty strange name for a gal."

"Well, Daddy, she picked that up on her first trip to Belize year's ago. She works with one of the locals and helped him build up his fishing business by partnering with him on a new boat. He dubbed her 'Ghetto Girl'."

"I heard there is some great fishing to be had down there in

Belize my darling daughter."

"So they say, Daddy, so they say."

The stench from the night before had finally begun to dissipate at the ice house. A cool morning breeze blew through the open garage doors and seemed to bring a little bit of life back into the bar. A couple of locals, sitting by the jukebox, were arguing over whether the Texans or the Cowboys were a better football team. They both seemed to have their own strong opinion. Ouida walked over to their table.

"What you guys hollerin' about so early for?"

"Ah Ouida, just a little bit of competitive banter goin' on. Nothin' for your pretty little head to worry about."

"Ok, then, can I get you guys anything?"

"Yeah, we will each take a jar of that crystal clear you got. Can you put it in a paper bag to go please?"

"Two to go guys. That'll be twenty bucks."

"If that shit wasn't so good, I would fight you on the price Ouida."

"Yeah, well you can't get a fifth of nothin' that good for that price around here mister."

Ouida walked to the back room of the bar, sacked up two jars of moonshine and returned to her customers. They exchanged money and headed out the door.

"Was en da werld yew inten ta doooo wif all dat imbentory

yew got in dat dar office Ouida?"

"I am a woman of means now Joe. I can't expect to make a living just off this bar. Besides, one day I'll be too old to have to worry about this stuff. Just consider that inventory my retirement package."

"As lung as I be alive I sho hadn't seen nuffin' like this 'round here goin' on. Gots ta be ver careful wit dat stuff nah Ouida."

"Joe, I can always count on you to care about my business ventures. I'll definitely keep this on the down low."

Thanksgiving Moonshine

A few weeks passed and Tater's business plan was moving along as expected. She was receiving deliveries from three states now and refining the product for resale. Her crew was doing a bang up job and she couldn't be happier. The last of the pecan trees in the orchard across the road were shedding their remaining leaves indicating the conclusion of fall in the river bottom. The air was cool and crisp bringing memories of the holidays to Tater's mind. She was excited that Thanksgiving was right upon them and had organized something special for the entire gang. Tater asked the crew to join her on the front porch.

"I want to thank everyone for what you have done to help me grow this business. Your dedication to our mission, your hard work and fantastic customer service is key to what we do around here. We are entering the holiday season and with Thanksgiving happening the end of this week, I want to add something special to your tables as a way of my saying 'Thank you' for all that you do."

Tater walked over to a refrigerated truck she had parked out front and motioned everyone to follow her. As she opened the back door, everyone's eyes went wide with surprise.

"On your way out, please take one of the Yeti coolers in

here. I think you will find what you need for a wonderful Thanksgiving feast. Everything from turkey and dressing to the Goode and Co. pecan pie and homemade Blue Bell vanilla ice cream. Y'all have a wonderful Thanksgiving and we will see the crew back here bright and early Monday morning!"

Everyone took turns giving Tater a big hug although she wasn't really the hugging type. All she could do was submit to the loving and try to hide the blush creeping around that freckled face of hers.

Tater awoke Thanksgiving morning at her daddy's house. The aroma of fresh brewed Folger's coffee and homemade cinnamon rolls were too tempting to stay in bed a minute longer.

"Well, hello there baby doll. You simply look marvelous this morning my darling daughter."

"Ah Daddy, I bet you say that to all the girls. Where in the world did you get these wonderful cinnamon rolls? I know cooking is not your forte."

"Well, darlin', Dwanna Crabb brought these by yesterday as her way of sayin' Happy Thanksgiving. She said it was a little 'gift of love' to you and me."

"Is that right? Now Daddy, you know that Dwanna is real sweet on you."

"Not to change the subject Tater, but we are going to head out to our local Turkey Day spot and feed the community. Polk and San Jacinto counties combined their feasts this year and it should be a humdinger."

Tater poured herself a fresh cup of joe and hastily dove into one of the fresh, hot, icing-oozed cinnamon rolls. Murphy made them both a to-go mug of coffee and filled a Coleman thermos for the trip over to Coldspring. Tater stuck two additional cinnamon rolls in a paper bag and they both headed out the door.

Tater and her daddy reached the Coldspring town square early on that crisp November morning. The sky was bright blue and the trees had voluntarily shed their leaves providing a blanket of amber, gold and orange throughout the square. It was simply an inviting sight. She loved participating in the community Thanksgiving event every year.

Tater ran into Dwanna over at the turkey carving station.

"Dwanna, you really get around don't you?"

"Well, we need to do what we can for everyone around here Tater. There's so many in our own backyard who is hungry and don't have a place to go for a wonderful Thanksgiving meal. The great thing here is we have had some blessed contributions this year to make this event the best ever."

"Is that so?"

"Why thank the Lord it sure is Tater Murphy! We had a couple of local businessmen, who have asked to remain anonymous, provide fifty-dollar prepaid Visa cards to each family who shows up today in need. This will go such a long way and may help each of their Christmases be a bit brighter! Oh Hallelujah! I just almost can't contain myself!"

"Well, hallefreakinlujah Dwanna!"

"And another thing, the local farmers donated ten percent of their harvest to the event. They never done that before and evidently Mr. Lobo had made his rounds and persuaded the farmers co-op to participate. He even put his down home charming pressure on those who had their own personal gardens to contribute. He and Mrs. Carol donated a portion of their harvest as well. So we truly have us a banquet from the Lord here today! A true loaves and fishes miracle!"

"Well, Dwanna, point me in the right direction and I'll get started."

"Sure, Tater, follow me. Will that sweet daddy of yours need some direction as well today?"

Tater giggled and shrugged her shoulders.

Dwanna led Tater over to the serving area and paired her up with attorney Elizabeth Mayhaw in dishing up the main course. The spread was amazing. There were pounds of carved turkey, homemade stuffing, rich thick gravy, green bean and sweet potato casseroles, mashed potatoes, cranberry dressing, deviled eggs, hot Parker House rolls and an array of desserts made by many of the ladies in the county. The banquet literally wrapped around the town square. The local police department was directing traffic and coordinating the influx of diners at noon that day. One of the highlights was a local band who had the best Hammond B-3 organist around. He was the highlight of the entire show. Funny thing is, he is the choir director at Dwanna's church and could definitely run rings around the best of the best with the way he played that organ. They literally had them a Thanksgiving party out on the plaza. It was amazing to see how many folk came out to volunteer their love, time, hard work and passion for those in need. It was a festive time had by all. The crowd was on its best behavior and everyone got a gut full.

Right about quitting time, the law pulled up with their sirens blaring. Everyone ran to the West side of the square to see what was going on. Sheriff Jess was outfitted in full regalia and had stopped his vehicle in front of the diner across the street.

"Margaret, did you really think you were going to get away with this? You have a very family friendly restaurant and you somehow thought another line of business might bring you in more cash?"

"Well, Sheriff, with the recession and everything, we had to do something. We didn't cause no one no harm. We were just able to provide a unique product to our paying customers. Surely you understand Sheriff, surely!"

Sheriff Jess and his deputies handcuffed Margaret and her crew and read them their Miranda rights, packing them into two of the patrol cars. After they were hauled off, a couple of officers wheeled three dollies out of the diner stacked with unlabeled cardboard boxes packed with moonshine filled mason jars and loaded them into their patrol cars. Apparently, there was a moonshine racket that had made it's way into Coldspring. The folks being arrested didn't put up much of a fuss and Sheriff Jess didn't look pleased at all. Suffice it to say, Thanksgiving was not immune to the moonshine outbreak.

Later that afternoon, Cherokee and Patty dropped by Mr. Lobo's and Mrs. Carol's place for some turkey dinner and football with the entire family. The Houston Texans were playing and Mrs. Carol made damn sure dinner was ready to go before the game began. You see, Mrs. Carol was the biggest Houston Texans fan there ever was on the face of this earth. Of course Mr. Lobo always took credit for teaching her all about football but she took this spectator sport to an entirely new level for a sexy senior citizen. She may not be a big talker day to day, but get her in front of that boob tube during a Texans game and all bets were off! She called every player by name, understood every play they made and cussed them up one side and down the other with a filthy sailor mouth for every play they missed. It was quite a sight watching her tiny little body hop up outta her recliner and fly at the television screen hurling fists and other colorful verbiage at the spectacle. Her family was convinced the players could hear her through the television. Most of those who came to watch the game were really there to observe momma coach and cuss the players.

Halftime came around and everyone was ready for either a smoke on the porch or a quick cold one. All were sitting around in a comatose state as a result of the wonderful dinner they ate earlier. Cherokee pulled a mason jar out and screwed off the lid. Mr. Lobo could smell the stuff across the porch and looked at Cherokee.

"That doesn't smell like any artesian water from around here Cherokee."

Cherokee shook his head no and tried to hand the jar over to Mr. Lobo for a swig. Right about that time Mrs. Carol opened the screen door, stepped outside and looked at Mr. Lobo with a "You better the hell not take a taste of that!" look. So Mr. Lobo waved his hand at Cherokee and said, "No thank ya, gotta keep my wits about me tonight."

OUIDA'S GIFT

December had been an extremely busy month for Tater, Cueball and Patty. They were reaching capacity with processors one and two and would soon need to tap into processor three by the end of the first quarter next year. Tater had eight sludge trucks coming in each day and two tankers going out regularly every afternoon. This kept Cueball and Patty very busy. So much so that Cueball was working late into the evening each night making sure all the equipment was running well and the Texas Tea tankers were prepped for filling and delivery the next day. He told Patty that he would cover this part of the work as it was his job as Logistics Manager to do so. It was enough that she was working ten-hour days and so he would take up the slack. He was putting in a ton of overtime but made sure to take Sundays off. He didn't complain, however, because he loved what he was doing and had learned more about technology and sludge processing than he could have ever imagined. He was thankful that Tater took him under her wing and made sure he understood everything about the business and trusted him with it when she was away. He also never imagined he would be running a crew. Patty and the truckers that operated Texas Tea's tankers were loyal and worked just as hard as he did. Life really couldn't be any better for him. He was doing well, making enough money to keep him out of trouble and was able to put some of it away to start thinking of getting some property and building a place of his own. Perhaps, one day, he dreamed of marrying Sallie Jean and settling down. But he knew it would be a ways off before that would happen.

Every evening after locking up the property, Cueball would head on home. He had no need to go into town and get into anyone else's business unless, of course, he was hungry for some pie. He and Sallie Jean were staying in touch but nothing very serious had become of them quite yet on account of their differing schedules. They would go into Livingston and catch a movie every Sunday and have a bite to eat at either Shrimp Boat Manny's or El Burrito Mexican Restaurant. However, this did not equate to a serious relationship for them. Serious, down in the river bottom, is when someone shacks up with the other person. Shacking up did not equate to a formal marriage arrangement but certainly had its own set of rules when it came to a mutual respect for the shack agreement. Cueball and Sallie Jean had not even considered that option yet. They were just running around like high school sweethearts all goo-goo eyed and causing a stir amongst the gossiping community.

Cueball drove on home that evening and parked his truck in the driveway. Mr. Lobo was out in his garden turning off the sprinklers and shouted over to Cueball motioning for him to come on over. Cueball waved and headed over.

"Hey Cue! Come on in and sit a spell with Mrs. Carol and myself. We would love to know how things are going for you over at Tater's operation."

Cueball followed Mr. Lobo into the house.

"Come on out on the back porch here Cueball, we can drink a beer and catch up for a few."

They all sat around and shot the shit while tossing back a few Old Milwaukee Lights.

Mrs. Carol handed Cueball another beer and said, "Tell us about the job Cue."

"Mrs. Carol, it's the best thing that has ever happened to me in my entire life. Tater runs a tight ship and I'm in charge of logistical matters running the machinery, processing the oil and managing Patty and the trucking crew."

"Well, that's mighty fine Cue. What about that sweet little Sallie Jean we've been hearing all about?"

Cueball turned red, looked down towards the ground and fiddled with his ear.

"She's the sweetest thing I have ever known. We have been friends since we wuz kids. I see her most every Sunday."

Mr. Lobo shouted out, "Well, that's wonderful Cue! It's good to know you found yourself a catch! You will have to bring her over sometime for dinner."

"We haven't gotten too serious at this point yet. I need

time to save up more money to get an official place of my own. Then, I will take our relationship to the next level."

As they kicked back on the porch, they noticed a UPS truck head towards Robin Lane. Cueball looked at Mr. Lobo.

"Have you ever seen a UPS truck come down here this late at night Mr. Lobo?"

"Nope, we sure haven't Cue. However, come to think of it, we are nearing the Christmas season and maybe those late night deliveries are starting to kick off again. It does make one wonder."

After a couple hours, Cueball decided it was best for him to head on home. As he walked up the steps of the front porch he found a mason jar full of water and a note that read, "Miss you, Love Ouida." He took the mason jar inside and set it on his kitchen counter. He then hopped into the shower to wash the day off. Next, he pulled on his pajamas and sat in his Lazy Boy recliner flipping on the TV DVR to watch a taped episode his favorite show "Survivor". He kept looking over at the jar wondering what the hell Ouida was up to but tried to think nothing of it intending to return it to her the following day. His curiosity ended up getting the best of him so he decided to open the jar and determine what that water was. He walked over to the counter and screwed the lid off then stepped back at the potency of the alcohol that was inside. He lifted it to his nose and realized this definitely wasn't rubbing alcohol. He took a little sip and thought, "As potent smelling as this is, it sure tastes darn smooth."

"Beep! Beep! Beep!" the alarm wailed. The sound nearly tossed Cueball out of bed when he heard it. He grabbed his head and looked over at his nightstand only to find the empty mason jar sitting there. He ran to the bathroom, grabbed a packet of BC Powder and chucked it into a cold glass of water, promptly drinking it once dissolved. He put on a pot of coffee and drank a cup as he got ready for work. Deciding he needed to make a quick stop before arriving at the shop, Cueball drove out to Ouida's icehouse and returned the empty mason jar placing it on Ouida's porch with a note attached that read, "Don't miss you, stay the fuck away! Cue." Cueball headed back to work and walked into Tater's office.

"You look like a damn truck hit you!"

"Yeah, well, a friend dropped off some homemade whiskey on my doorstep last night and I had a bit too much before I hit the hay. Thank God my alarm was set before I decided to drink most of it."

Tater laughed. "Go get yourself some coffee and let's take a look at today's schedule."

SHERIFF JESS

Mr. Lobo and Murphy were sitting on the front porch of the feed store shooting the breeze as they did just about every morning. They called it their "solving the world's problems" session. Mr. Lobo had a cigarette in his mouth and a coffee cup in his hand. This was routine for him as long as it was before five pm every day. Anything past five required a few adult beverages. Murphy was chewin' on a Swisher Sweet and enjoyed coffee with his smoke as well. They were permanent fixtures around town and all the old guys in the county would drop in now and then to see if there was anything new to share with one another. This particular cool December morning was different from most. The air was thin with a light East Texas winter breeze. The sky was a dismal gray and the pecan trees had gone to sleep for the season. Instead of talking about the usual harvest, the damn war that seemed to never end and climate change, a new item had ended up on their agenda.

"Murph, you hear anything about moonshine down here in San Jacinto County?"

"Nope, why Lobo?"

"Well, I was talkin' with some neighbors the other night and one of them pulled out a mason jar and he took a swig. I looked at him and said, 'that ain't no water from no artesian well around here now is it?' He looked at me and shook his head no. Then he proceeded to pass me the jar and I didn't have to taste it because the smell of 100% proof filled the atmosphere. Mrs. Carol looked at me and gave me one of those loving 'I'm going to beat you if you taste that' looks so I waved my hand and said, 'No thank ya.' I asked him where he got it and he said he would have to kill me if he told me."

"Where do you think he got the white lightning Lobo?"

"I don't really know, but Mrs. Carol and I have decided to keep a greater eye out for suspicious characters around the neighborhood. The only thing we have really noticed is a new UPS driver visiting our neck of the woods. It's Christmas and so I guess that warrants another driver. The same gal who's been delivering to us for years is also running her truck down in the river bottom. She would usually have a helper on the truck and there would be no need for another delivery driver to come down here in another UPS truck. Not sure if that is significant but it sure does make us wonder."

"I'll have to do a little asking around also. Tater may have heard something and, if not, Dwanna always has the dirt."

"My old buddy Sam Wade, who lives off the infamous Highway 59 and runs the vegetable stand, has a real neat surveillance setup on his property. I might just set something up on mine just to keep an eye on the road at night after we have gone to bed."

"Well, if anyone in this county can figure out what's going on, we certainly have had a great track record for doing so."

Mr. Lobo nodded his head in agreement and they turned back to the world's other problems for the day.

Mr. Lobo's cellphone rang and he answered it.

"Hello Sam, were your ears burnin'? I was just talkin' about you."

"Oh yeah? Did you take a look at the paper today? Remember the other night when Cherokee brought that jar of moonshine over to your place? Well, pick up the paper and read the police blotter. It's not every day that you hear about moonshine in the county within the same twenty-four hour period!"

With that, Mr. Lobo hung the phone up and asked Murphy if he had a paper handy. Murphy reached down beside his chair and passed it over to him.

"Well, I'll be damn. Take a look at this Murphy."

Murphy looked under the police blotter section of the paper and it read, "A group of high schoolers were caught behind the community center on Friday night drinking jars of moonshine. When asked where they got it, they did not reveal any information. The teens were taken into custody for further questioning and charged with mischievous looting and drinking under the age."

"We definitely need to keep an eye out around here. There's something going on and it needs to be gotten to the bottom of Lobo."

"Well, this is going to be a real rabble rouser once the shit hits the fan down here in old San Jac. I'll definitely be keepin' an eye out and snoopin' around my part of the county."

Mr. Lobo headed back home and fired up his CB radio base station. Mrs. Carol entered his office. She stood about five foot eight, thinner than your little finger, long sandy blonde hair and as weathered as a Cherokee squaw in the summertime. She had this honey glow about her and a look of suspicion dancing across her face.

"Lobo, why are you gettin' on that damn thing again? I don't ever get any time with you because of that electronic device."

"Now honey, we got a mystery to solve down here in the river bottom and I need your help with this too!"

Mrs. Carol shook her fist at Mr. Lobo and marched out of the room in a tizzy.

Mr. Lobo picked up the handset to his base station.

"Breaker breaker 1-9, anyone copy, this here's Papa Bear."

"Hey Papa Bear! This is Captain. I got your twenty."

"Hey Captain, got anything coming up on the bear band about some tomato sauce around here?"

"Negatory, ain't heard nothin' but seeing a bunch of Kojaks with a Kodak out here on the road today."

"Well, let's keep Black Bart out of this in case we find Bears with Ears On."

"10-4 good buddy, will keep you posted. Got some Beaver Fever. Headed home off this flip flop. Over and out."

"Over and out."

"That you Papa Bear?"

"That's a 10-4 Cherokee."

"Got some more of that tater sauce if you are interested. Home grown good from the ground."

"Negatory, we got a whole garden full of maters here. However, you got any information on that milk run we talked about the other night Cherokee?"

"Negatory Papa Bear. I'll keep my eye out for the candy store though."

"Momma's callin', Over."

"Tell her I said hello Papa Bear. Over."

Things started getting awfully suspicious around the county. Everyone knew about the moonshine racket by now but no one was saying a thing. Every once in a while someone would flub up and ask, "Got any of that 'WL' or know where I can find some?" So you knew what they were talkin' about because folks down here can be so damn stupid when it comes to secrecy.

Particularly when it involves illegal hooch being passed underground.

Sheriff Jess was having a fit because every arrest he made consisted of either high school kids who would turn around and accuse their least favorite teacher of giving it to them or old women blaming their next door neighbors of having a supply which most of the time ended up being unfounded.

The local Family Dollar owner was arrested because he had an entire rack of the stuff in his back storage room. An old lady tipped the sheriff off when she saw him carry a "stinky box" back to the storage area. When questioned, the owner stated that he had simply found the box on his front stoop when opening up one day and decided to go put it in the back until he could figure out what it was.

The biggest bust was down at the tire store when the sheriff made his weekly visit just to check in on things. He found every customer in the waiting area with a jar in their hand. Needless to say, they were promptly taken down to the pokey. They all blamed the tire shop owner who was promptly arrested as well and ultimately his business was shut down. The sheriff asked the tire shop owner where he got the hooch and he said he just found it on his back stoop one day and since he didn't drink, he was going to share it with his loyal customers.

Sheriff Jess was about fed up with hitting brick walls and stupid leads. Suspicion was getting the best of him and he decided he was going to find the culprit if it took him until the new year to do so. He set out on his mission and began visiting every courthouse, community center, law office, gas station, post office, church, sawmill, tattoo parlor, diner, feed store and grocer in the county asking about suspicious packages and particularly suspicious beverages.

Christmas Investigation

Christmas Eve arrived and Ouida's icehouse which boomed with honky tonk music and drunken laughter. In walked the tall drink of water Ouida could never get her claws into. She admired his authoritative brown county mountie uniform that seemed to accentuate his muscular physique. Sheriff Jess walked over to the bar, twisting his handlebar moustache he looked over at Ouida.

"Well, hello there Ouida Mae. Merry Christmas! It sure has been a while."

"Yes, it has Sheriff. Too long. What brings you here tonight? Can I buy you a beer and you sit a spell with us?"

Coon-Ass Joe looked up from the bar, belched and walked off to the men's room. Gomer followed close behind. You could tell everyone in the bar was getting geared up for the night's celebration and didn't need the likes of the sheriff in there.

"Well, no thank you Ouida. I'm here on official business. I would like you to keep an eye out for me tonight in the event you have anyone bringing in or trying to sell you any of that white lightning that is being passed around the county. There is a reward if we get any leads on who is distributing this stuff."

The Sheriff made his proclamation as loudly as possible. As a result, heads turned and took note of what he had just said.

"What is the reward? A date with you?"

"Ha ha, no, but you can bet we have a couple grand in this reward that will make it worthwhile for someone to come forward."

"Sure would make a nice Christmas bonus Sheriff. I'll keep an eye out for you. How would you like to drop by for a beer when you get off tonight? I'm buyin!"

"No thank you Ouida, but I appreciate the offer."

With that, Sheriff Jess tipped his Stetson, turned and headed on out the door.

Sheriff Jess pounded the pavement that evening and visited Sallie Jean's Diner, the Masonic Lodge, JT's Gas and Grocery, Charlie's Burger Joint, Church's Chicken, and Zeke's Drive-In before it got too late. By the time he reached his last destination of the night, word spread like wildfire all over the county about the reward out for the hooch dealer. Dispatch radioed the sheriff and told him to get into the office as soon as he could.

As the sheriff entered the station, there was a waiting room full of locals lining up to talk to him. He scratched his head and walked over to the deputy at the counter. The deputy leaned over the counter.

"They're here about the reward."

The sheriff turned to the crowd.

"Folks, I want to thank you for coming down here on Christmas Eve and all. However, I want you to know that although we do have a reward out for the hooch dealer, we won't be paying out the reward until the person is apprehended."

Sighs could be heard throughout the room. Most of the crowd got up and exited the building with the exception of a few who stayed behind thinking it couldn't hurt if they catch the person they suspect is up to it. The sheriff looked at those who remained and told them someone would be in to take their statements shortly. Visitors, with so-called leads, flooded the station every day between Christmas and New Year's. The sheriff made three trips a day into the waiting area to make the "We don't pay out until. . ." speech and only those who truly thought they might know something would stick around.

The following morning, Sheriff Jess decided to make a trip to Tater's business. He rapped on her office door.

"Come in!"

"Hey Tater Baby, how you doin'?"

"Hey Uncle Jess! All's good around here. Heard you're on the hunt for someone haulin' moonshine around the county. Have you found the bootlegger yet?"

"Nope, that's why I'm here Tater. I figure with all those truckers that come in through here, someone surely knows somethin' about the traffickin' goin' on."

"Well, I haven't heard anything out in the yard about this but, to be honest, I haven't thought about asking. Uncle Jess, let me see what I can find out and if it seems like there's something to it, I'll definitely call you first!"

"That's my gal! Thank you so much. Tell that brother of mine I said hello and can't wait to see you all on New Year's for bar-b-cue out at the house."

"Sure thing, Uncle Jess. You be careful out there!"

Later that afternoon, Tater stepped out into the yard to have a chat with a couple of her drivers.

"Hey guys, can you keep an ear out for information leading to the county moonshiner?"

One of the drivers waved to Tater and said, "Will keep an eye out Tater. Surely something will come up sooner or later."

Tater looked over at Cueball and Patty and motioned them to come into the office.

"Sit down you two, I need to talk to you about something."

Cueball and Patty looked at each other puzzled and sat right down. Tater picked up the candy jar off her desk and leaned it towards the two.

"Jawbreaker?"

Cueball and Patty shook their heads no.

"Now, I know you both have really worked hard since our

opening and want you to know that it does not go unnoticed. Now that we are nearing the end of the year, I want to give you a token of my appreciation for doing such an amazing job so far!"

Tater handed them both an envelope that contained a ten percent pay bonus as a thank you for the job well done. Cueball and Patty were grinning from ear to ear. Neither one of them had ever received a bonus for doing a good job. In fact, they didn't know such a thing actually existed.

"Thank you!" rang from both of their mouths in unison.

Tater smiled.

"You deserve it! Now, I do have one other thing I need you to do for me."

"What's that Tater?"

"Well, Cue, you remember that homemade whiskey you said someone left on your stoop a while ago?"

Cueball nodded his head yes.

"That was actually moonshine and there is an illegal moonshine operation going on somewhere in the county. Uncle Jess is looking for those involved and hasn't had any great leads yet. Well, I think we can keep talking to our drivers to find out if they know anything and maybe, just maybe, we can help Uncle Jess out. You OK with that?"

"Absolutely!" exclaimed Cueball.

Patty nodded her head yes in agreement.

"Great! That makes me feel like we are doing our part for

the community also."

Right about that time Coon-Ass Joe came stumbling in the door. Cueball helped him to a chair because he looked more frazzled than ever.

"Mah deer Gomah dun dit croaked en dah lawn outside ya drive out dah."

Coon-Ass Joe pointed out the door. Cueball ran out the door and into the parking lot scooping Gomer up realizing that he wasn't dead, he was just passed out drunk.

"Well, Joe, it appears your dear Gomer is a bit more inebriated than normal and simply needs to go home and sleep it off. How 'bout I give you both a ride home? I'm finished up here for the day."

Coon-Ass Joe was crying tears of drunken joy when he realized Gomer was passed out and not dead. He accepted the lift from Cueball and he and Gomer headed on home.

New Year's Tip

New Year's Eve was the best night for any of the grown folk in the county. It was a great babysitting opportunity for the young girls in the area as well. They could count on making good money on New Year's Eve so the older couples could go out and kick their heels up. The local boys had a stake in New Year's Eve activities also. They had their truck winches primed and ready to pull any fool out of a mud hole or ditch due to being a bit more tipsy than expected. Many of them hung out in front of the local clubs and nabbed the stumblers persuading partiers to be chauffeured home for a nominal fee.

The only place in Shepherd to celebrate was Ouida's icehouse where the locals hung out. That crowd was not the type of folk Tater cared to hang out with on New Year's Eve. So, Tater met the gang out at Cherokee's house off FM 1127. Cherokee held his annual New Year's Eve party at his place. His homestead was a single-wide trailer that he built a house around, following Mr. Lobo's example, and sat on a nice flat acre parcel. Cherokee sure did do the place up. He had a huge outdoor covered patio. Inside he had built himself a game room with a pool table, bar and hi-fi system that you could hear halfway across the county.

Tater walked into the haze of smoke from all kinds of "natural herbs" as well as the echo of Journey playin' over Cherokee's booming sound system.

"Hey there Tater gal! It's about time you showed up in here! We were waitin' for you to get this damn party started."

"Hey Cherokee! You know I could never miss your New Year's Eve hoedown!"

With that, Tater moved across the room and found Cueball and Sallie Jean smoochin' in the corner.

"Ahem. Happy Almost New Year you love bugs!"

Cueball and Sallie Jean hopped up and gave Tater a big hug.

"Happy New Year to you too Tater Murphy!"

Sallie Jean gave Tater another hug.

"Carry on my waaayward son" blared over the speakers.

Tater felt a tap on her shoulder and turned around.

"Hi cutie! How you doin'? I haven't seen you since the day you brought Cue over to your daddy's trailer."

"I know Mrs. Carol. It has been too long. I need to make a habit of droppin' by more often. You know you and Mr. Lobo are my favorites down here in the river bottom."

"You know you're just sayin' that. I have to tell you though, I am so damn proud of you girl! You are such a strong, brave gal openin' up that business of yours in a land of testosterone thicker than mud on a stormy spring day. You're makin' a great name for us gals here in San Jacinto County. You should be just as proud of yourself too!"

"Well, thank you Mrs. Carol. That means so much to me and I promise, I won't let you or any of the other ladies in town down!"

"Back in Black, I hit the sack" echoed through the air as Tater turned and headed to the other end of the game room.

"Hey, Mr. Lobo. Just had a chat with your lovely wife over there. You better not let that one out of your sight or someone's gonna sweep her off her feet by the end of the night."

"Tater Murphy, you darn well know that's my woman and ain't no one ever gonna change her mind about that. She's my soul mate through and through!"

Tater nodded her head in agreement.

"Drank a little drank, smoke a little smoke" rang out of the hi-fi and many of those present raised their beer can or lighter or "rolled cigarette" and echoed the lyric "Smoke a little smoke."

The place was packed with people that night. Every year Cherokee's party gets a little bit bigger. Cherokee walked over to Tater.

"You have any of that artesian water that has been making its way around town?"

"What do you mean artesian water?" Tater paused for a minute and said, "Ah, so you know about that moonshine do ya?"

"Uh may have heard something about it."

"You mean that stuff over there in Coon-Ass Joe's hand?"

Cherokee looked over at Coon-Ass Joe and smiled.

"Well, I do believe so."

"Where in the world are you guys getting that stuff from?"

"Joe said he got it from Ouida out at her place."

"Cherokee, I gotta tell you that if you are caught red-handed with that stuff it could really get you into big trouble. Uncle Jess has made this his top priority on finding who is distributing it out here. He's not too happy about it either because the school kids are getting their hands on it and causing a ton of shit down in town."

"I'll keep this on the down low and make sure my hands are clean. Thanks for the warning Tater."

"You can't hide those lyin' eyes" sang out and got everyone dancing inside and out the house. Tater decided it was time for her to make her way home so she made her rounds and gave everyone a Happy New Year's pat on the back and headed on out.

The next morning Tater headed over to Uncle Jess' for his annual New Year's Day festivities. Uncle Jess lived off the west bank of Lake Livingston. His property sprawled a nice twenty acres along the shoreline. As you drove up you would think you were entering the gateway of someone on the Lifestyles of the

Rich and Famous. Big ass iron fence surrounded his property with a solar powered gate that swung open after plugging in the pass code. He had laid a nice asphalt road down that led up to his two-story, 3500 square foot, lake cabin. The road was lined with Weeping Willows and scattered throughout his property were pecan trees spanning 100 years old. The place was beautiful. Custom built by his old buddy from high school. The structure was a monstrous log cabin with the warmth and feel of a hunters lodge inside. Jess loved hunting and fishing as much, if not more, than his day job. He had evidence of this all over his walls. Huge bass, trout and even a sailfish mounted up high. Over the fireplace he had mounted a moose head from a Canadian hunt he went on three years ago. Over his patio door was the rack of a ten point buck he shot right out his back door last fall. Standing around staring at these magnificent creatures one would expect the animals to step right out of the wall and walk on over to you.

The floor to ceiling living room windows opened up to Lake Livingston and displayed the most beautiful views in all the area. Outside was a custom outdoor kitchen equipped with all the latest amenities anyone could want for preparing a great feast. Decked out with a Discovery 52-inch built-in outdoor stainless steel grill, Santa Cecilia granite countertops and a wet bar to satisfy the grownups present. All of this sat atop a huge patio accented with a green Muller roof overhang. Walk a few hundred feet off his back porch, toward the lake, and you reach the boat dock, cleaning station and mini water park he had built for his kids and grandkids. Two slides anchored the dock and attached to it were all kinds of kayaks, paddle boats, jet skis and wind surfers for all the kids at heart. A floating deck with a springboard was anchored between the dock and the channel marker.

Sheriff Jess had a heart of gold when it came to his family and those close to him. You could always count on him righting a wrong and making sure he was doing the best he could for the community. He wasn't one of your typical kickback cops like we have down here. He was honest through and through and no one could ever put one over on him. I reckon that is why he became Sheriff. He definitely had good karma going for him.

Tater walked in, gave him and Aunt Judy big hugs and kissed them both on the cheek. She wished them a Happy New Year and asked her Uncle Jess if she could have a minute with him. Uncle Jess and Tater took a walk out to the backyard.

"I think I might have a lead for you Uncle Jess."

"A lead Tater?"

"Well, I was at a party last night and someone actually had a jar of that moonshine that's circulating around the county. I asked one of the folks at the party where they got it from."

"And what did they say?"

"Well, they said that Ouida might know more about who is

distributing this stuff on account they got it from her."

"Oh my God! And it was right under my nose Christmas Eve when I went by to pay her a visit."

"Well, I don't think she's making it Uncle Jess. I just think she may be sharing it, if you know what I mean."

"Yes, true. I guess I know where my first stop will be in the morning. It can surely wait til then."

The remainder of the day was filled with family, black-eyed peas, cabbage, cornbread and a few briskets to keep the crowd happy.

Hysterical Marker

The next morning, on the way to the station, Sheriff Jess stopped by Ouida's icehouse to have a little chat. As he stepped inside, Ouida looked up.

"Now what have I done to deserve the pleasure of you dropping by so soon again Sheriff?"

"Well, Ouida, I have some business with you."

"Well, sit down, let's have it Sheriff."

The sheriff sat down next to Coon-Ass Joe and gave Gomer a pat on the head and offered him a dog bone out of his pocket.

"That thing doesn't look like he's eaten in days."

"No, he doesn't eat much anymore since his wife died," whispered Ouida.

"Well, I really wasn't talkin' about Joe, but now that you mention it, him too."

"Ok, what can I do you for Sheriff?"

"You know I have been working hard at finding that bootlegger down here in the county?"

Ouida nodded her head yes and leaned forward, elbows on the counter and chin in her hands gawkin' away at the sheriff.

"Well, Ouida, I have it on good authority that you may

have some information on where the moonshine might be coming from."

Ouida's chin slipped off her hands and darn near hit the bar before she could right herself.

"How the hell would I know where that stuff came from Sheriff? I haven't seen a lick of that stuff round here."

"Well, I beg to differ Ouida, because before I came in to talk to you I took a look around your property and found a couple of suspicious jars with some clear, potent liquid in them."

"Well, you can't prove those are mine! Because I don't even drink hard liquor no way!"

Coon-Ass Joe looked over at Ouida and gave her a bloodshot wink.

"Now Ouida, do I need to get a search warrant or are you just going to come out and share what you know with me?"

Right about that time Coon-Ass Joe picked his head up off the bar and pointed at Ouida.

"She don't know war dat dar stuff comes frum Sherf. . .but it shore duz taste gud!"

Coon-Ass Joe burped, farted and laid his head back on the bar.

Sheriff Jess frowned at Ouida.

"I'll give you a couple of days to come to your senses, otherwise, I'll come shut this place down for good Ouida!"

With that he got up and headed off to the station.

Ouida couldn't believe what had just happened. Her days of making a little extra money on the side were clearly near over, unless she could change her business model. She also wondered who in the hell told the Sheriff about her knowledge of the white lightning. Then it dawned on her. She picked up the phone, dialed Dwanna's number and the answering machine picked up.

"Hello, you have reached Dwanna. The rapture has taken me or I'm off runnin' a few errands. Please leave your name at the beep and I'll get back with you soon. Remember, Jesus Loves You and I do too! Beeeep."

"Dwanna! I need to TALK TO YOU IMMEDIATELY!"

Ouida hung up the phone and glared at Coon-Ass Joe. Coon-Ass Joe looked up at her, looked down at Gomer, got up and headed to the men's room.

"Make sure you hit the goddamn toilet this time Joe! I'm tired of cleaning up your nasty ass misses!"

She was definitely fit to be tied and couldn't wait to talk to Dwanna.

"Deirdre, I'll be back in a couple of hours. Take care of the shop while I'm gone."

"Sure will Ouida Mae."

Ouida ran out the back, pulled her van up to the door and began moving her hooch stock to her vehicle. She figured she needed to at least get the evidence out before the sheriff came by again. Ouida hopped into her van and sped down US 59 back into Shepherd and over to Dwanna's house to sit and wait for her to get home.

Dwanna pulled into the driveway about an hour later. She got out of her 1978 powder blue Cadillac Seville and walked over to Ouida.

"Dwanna, we've got to talk."

"Well, help me get my groceries in the house and we can chat."

Ouida and Dwanna toted sacks of groceries from the local Brookshire Brothers into the house. While Dwanna was unloading her groceries, Ouida came in carrying a box. Dwanna looked at her puzzled.

"What's in the box Ouida?"

"Take a look, I've got more outside."

Ouida went back to the van and Dwanna poked her head in the box jumping quickly back in amazement.

"Good Lord, Sweet Mother of God! Ouida!"

As Ouida returned, Dwanna looked at her confused.

"What are you doing bringing all this over to my house?"

"This is the only place people won't look for this stuff!"

"You can't leave that moonshine here Ouida! I would sure get into a lot of trouble if someone found out that I was hiding it here! I would be kicked off the quilting bee, shunned from the

Tabernacle, dear Lord knows what else! GET THAT OUT OF MY HOUSE NOW!"

Ouida froze in place because she never heard Dwanna get upset like that before.

"Dwanna, I have no place else to take this stuff!"

"Why don't you go put it in a storage locker outside the county until the dust settles?"

"Well, that's definitely a good idea. Can I keep this here just for one night?"

"OK, just one night. Now sit down and tell me why all this is happening."

"It has been one shit fall kind of day Dwanna. I don't even know where the hell to begin! First thing this mornin' that handsome damn Sheriff Jess came in asking me what I knew about this fuckin' bootlegger. He said someone told him that I knew the guy and where he could fuckin' find him. Funny thing is, I don't know shit about the guy. All I know is I put a certain amount of money in a jar on the back stoop of my bar each night and in the morning there's a case of this shit waitin' for me. I have no idea what the person looks like, where this shit comes from, nothin'. I'm just sad I had another source of income that obviously is not long lived at this point. I'll be by tomorrow to pick this stuff up and take it to storage. I can always wheel and deal in another county. Not sure how I'll handle future deliveries though. Dwanna, you are the best damn friend a gal can fuckin' have. Gotta go."

Dwanna gave Ouida a hug and sent her on her way. She took the boxes and hid them under her four poster bed in the back room.

Ouida headed over to Dwanna's the following afternoon. She drove a van which was a hysterical marker of sorts in town. A 1970 Chevy custom van painted with the classic sunset oranges, yellows and browns on both sides. The special porthole window on the back of each side of the van was a clear indication of the era in which it was born. Plump Firestone radials accented with big whitewalls anchored the behemoth. An evacuation window, aka moon-roof, popped up on the top backside of the van. The iconic "Keep On Truckin" dude was painted on the back door of this special edition. His front sole kicked up and his thumb sticking out at those who tailed Ouida through town. She had a supercharged sound system with an outdated 8-track player tucked in the dash. The inside of the passenger area of the van was lined in deep brown and gold shag carpeting, a bench back couch and a mini fridge for those long hauls. On any typical day she would be driving down the road, windows rolled down and something from Led Zeppelin blaring out the windows for all to enjoy.

Ouida pulled into the driveway and tooted her horn. Dwanna appeared at the door and motioned for Ouida to come on in.

"Ouida, you should be very careful with this stuff. It'll bring you nothing but trouble Precious One."

"Dwanna, I know exactly what I'm doin'. I have a safe hiding place for it and can run this business out of the other county with no problem. I'm like a fuckin' gangster!"

"If that's what you want to think Ouida. I'll be prayin' the Spirit covers you and protects you even though this is illegal."

Ouida gathered the cases of moonshine and returned them to the back of her van. She was headed out to Livingston, over in Polk county, to drop the supplies at the local U-Haul storage center. As she drove down US 59, a big buck jumped into the middle of the highway and Ouida slammed on her breaks. "Boom!" Tires and glass went flying in one direction and the van went rolling in another. The deer was lodged in the front window of the van deader than a doornail. Ouida stepped out of the van dazed, her face scratched and bloodied, her clothes soaked in moonshine.

"Breaker breaker Papa Bear, you copy?"

"10-4 good buddy, what's your twenty?"

"Cruisin' down this here US 59 where a deer got caught in the lights and someone we both know is now belly up on the side of the road."

"Dear Lord, are they hurt Captain?"

"Negatory, just a little shook up. Interesting thing is County Mountie Jess is here and taking our friend Ouida into custody."

"Well, first off, you and I both know she ain't no friend of ours. And secondly, why the hell is she being taken to the pokey?"

"Not completely sure yet Papa Bear but it appears it has something to do with some alcohol they found in her van that shattered all the hell over the place when she hit that deer."

Mr. Lobo let out a huge laugh.

"That damn Ouida is a piece of work. I wonder if she might be the rum runner they been talkin' about around here for weeks now. I sure the hell wouldn't be surprised."

"I'll be home soon, let's solve some world problems in an hour or so. Over and out Papa Bear."

"Over and out Captain."

"Breaker Breaker Papa Bear, you copy? Seems like we got us a convoy up there on US 59 near the Lake Livingston cutoff."

"10-4 Veggie Man. Understand Ouida has gotten herself into a situation as she has pickled herself and her van with some illegal hooch."

"Uh oh. I wonder. . . ."

"Just what I was thinkin' Veggie Man, but it is just too clean of a break for Sheriff Jess. I just don't see where Ouida would have the wherewithal to pull something this big off. She probably was just selling the shit to make some money."

"True dat. Over and out Papa Bear."

"Over and out Veggie Man."

Mr. Lobo walked into the living room and found Mrs. Carol staring up at him.

"Well, what in the hell is going on with Ouida?"

Mr. Lobo laughed and explained to her what Clyde radioed about. Mrs. Carol shook her head and exclaimed, "Serves her nasty ass right!"

"You've got it all wrong Sheriff! I don't know how in the world that got in the back of my van! I was on my way to Wally World in Livingston and this deer came out of nowhere and blam! I ran smack dab into him and all these bottles went to shatterin' in the back of my van! I had no idea they were in there and definitely no idea where they came from. I sweeeeaaaaarrrrrr on my deeeeaaaadddd mommmmmaaaaas graaaveee!"

"Well, you are going to have to explain that to the judge Ouida. Can you tell me how that jar fit so squarely into your cup holder to begin with?"

"It must have lodged right in there when the van rolled over! I'm sure you will find my Dr. Pepper bottle somewhere on the floorboard. That's what I drink all day long, good ole D.P."

"They will take your statement at the station."

Sheriff Jess handcuffed Ouida.

"Watch your head, Ouida, we are going for a ride."

They arrived at the station and he escorted Ouida into the receiving area at which time a couple of folks pointed at her.

"Sheriff Jess! That's your whiskey runner! I recall seeing her hauling some stuff off to Polk County the other night!"

Sheriff Jess led Ouida to the fingerprinting station.

"Ouida, you will have a hearing with the judge first thing in the morning. You have one phone call and I recommend you find yourself a good lawyer."

The sheriff took Ouida's fingerprints and snapped a couple of mugshots. She was led to a holding cell where she would remain until it was time to go see the judge.

A payphone hung on the cell wall and Sheriff Jess promptly gave her a quarter to make her call.

"Ring ring ring, ring ring ring. Hello, this is Dwanna, I'm not here at the moment cuz the Lord sent me on a mission this afternoon. Please leave a message and I'll get back with you unless He takes me first. Remember, Jesus Loves You and I do too! Beeeeeeeep."

"I've about had enough of this bullshit answering machine crap trying to get ahold of you Dwanna! If you are there, please fuckin' pick up your piece of crap phone! I am in jail and I need your help immediately! Get over here as soon as you get this message!"

Ouida slammed the receiver against the payphone, threw

her hands up to her face and started to squall. All the other prisoners in the holding cell covered their ears as they had never heard such a thing in all their lives. Some were moved to want to either knock her head off to shut her up or bang their own heads against the wall so as to put them out of their misery.

A young girl approached Ouida. She smoothed out the sleeves on her blue mechanics shirt, walked over and put her arm around Ouida's shoulder.

"Hey girl, my name's Coco. I'm gonna take care of you in here. Don't you worry about a thing honey."

Ouida looked up relieved feeling she had already made a friend thinking that this Coco girl felt sorry for her because of her crying and all. Coco slapped her hand on Ouida's ass and Ouida jumped what seemed to be ten feet away.

"Mother Fuckin' Coco shit whatever your goddamn sonofabitch pussy eating name is, you better keep those skanky smellin' ass hands off of me or I'll. . ."

"Or you'll what? You think you can fuck with me you piece of shit white trash hooker ass?"

"Hooker ass? I'm no fuckin' STD catchin' hooker! You think I'm a hooker! What the mother fuckin' hell! You are one to talk in your baggy ass jeans, red bandana rapped gangsta head. What are you, the Taco Bell chihuahua or somethin'?"

Coco stepped closer to Ouida.

"I'll have you know that I just got arrested for traffickin' hooch in this county which, of course, I am not guilty of! I was in the wrong goddamn place at the wrong sonofabitchin' time!"

"Well, whatever the hell you are in here for now bitch, you are mine."

Ouida balled her hand into a fist, drew back and smacked Coco square in between her eyes. Coco fell to the ground and was out for the count. Ouida was grabbing her hand as she was sure it was broken and then kicked Coco in the gut for good measure. Sheriff Jess came around the corner due to the racket he heard down the hall. He called for a medic for Coco and pulled Ouida out and put her in another cell for safety precautions.

"Well, now you want to add aggravated assault to your charges Ouida?"

"Only if you add attempted rape to Coco's charges. She was sexually harassing me Sheriff! I've never!"

The next morning, Sheriff Jess visited Ouida's cell followed by Dwanna and another woman unfamiliar to Ouida.

"Ouida, you've got visitors."

He turned to Dwanna and her companion.

"Thirty minutes until she leaves to visit the judge so make it quick ladies."

The Sheriff left the room and Dwanna looked at Ouida and smiled.

"Ouida, this is my pastor's daughter Elizabeth Mayhaw. She's a lawyer out of Coldspring and she will be able to help you."

Elizabeth stuck her hand out to shake Ouida's and Ouida simply looked at her and spat on the ground.

"I don't need your goddamn charity whoever you are."

"Oh, this isn't charity Ms. Lawless. This is how I make a living so you will have to pay me cold hard cash to get your ass out of this pickle."

"You need to listen to Elizabeth, Ouida. She's the best criminal lawyer in town. She will be able to help you better than anyone else in the county."

Ouida sized up Elizabeth. She didn't stand much taller than Ouida. Her plump stature put her at about 250 pounds. Elizabeth grabbed the lapel of her Beall's brown polyester pantsuit.

"That sure is a pretty frilly satin pink blouse you got on there Ms. Mayhaw. Too bad you used it to wipe your mouth this morning during breakfast. You could have at least washed that mustard off before you came to visit me."

Elizabeth pulled out her handkerchief to wipe the sweat off her brow. Frustration reflected in her bulging eyes as she glared at Ouida.

"I'll remind you, Ms. Lawless, that I am here to get you out of this mess. I would highly advise you to keep your mouth shut until spoken to. It will do you a heck of a lot of good as we move through the next couple of hours."

"Well, what the hell have I got to lose?"

For twenty minutes the three ladies sat and talked about the events of the past couple of days.

"I honestly am a victim of circumstance! My van is a mess! How am I going to get that smell out of the rug?"

She left out the details about hiding the hooch at Dwanna's the night before.

"I will take your case if you could do one specific thing."

"What the fuck is that?"

"Just that!"

"Just the fuck what?"

"That you don't use any foul language in front of law enforcement, the judge or the District Attorney!"

"Oh hell, that's not going to be a shit problem for me. I know how to be fuckin' respectable in front of those goddamn muther fuckers."

Elizabeth looked at Dwanna who promptly shook her head from side to side, closing her eyes and sighing.

"I'm a real lady!" exclaimed Ouida.

Sheriff Jess entered the room.

"Time to go see the judge Ouida. You ladies also coming?"

The sheriff loaded Ouida up in his patrol car and headed to the Coldspring courthouse. Dwanna and Elizabeth followed close behind.

The bailiff walked across the marble floor as he moved to the front of the courtroom.

"All rise. The Superior Court of the State of Texas, County of San Jacinto, The Honorable Judge Marshall Watkins presiding, is now in session. Please be seated and come to order."

Ouida and Elizabeth stood at the defense's table and witnessed the entry of Judge Watkins as he arrived at his bench. His towering presence, combined with the long judges robe he wore was impressive and intimidating.

"You may be seated," his voice boomed.

This was your typical East Texas courtroom. The air in the room was thin and musky. A January coolness hugged the room. Judge Watkins took a seat. His bench was rich in detail. A bald eagle carved across the front and the words "In God We Trust" sprawled beneath the majestic bird. Both the state of Texas and United States flags flanked him on either side. Beside the bench sat a court reporter focused and pounding away on his stenography machine as the proceedings commenced.

"Ouida Mae Lawless, please rise."

Ouida and Elizabeth stood up out of respect for the court.

"You have been arrested for trafficking moonshine in San Jacinto County and aggravated assault. How do you plea?"

"Not guilty, your Highness."

Elizabeth snapped a look a Ouida and jabbed her in the side with her elbow.

"Uh, your Honorableness."

Elizabeth looked at her and whispered "Shuuuut uuuuup!"

"Your Honor, Ms. Lawless pleads not guilty to the trafficking charge and self defense to the aggravated assault charge. We would like to ask for supervised custody of her until her arraignment if it pleases the court."

"Attorney Mayhaw, as I always appreciate the sentiment held towards your defendants, I believe it behooves the court to retain Ms. Lawless until said trial begins. She is a danger to this community and has priors that allude to such. I will, however, set her bail at twenty thousand dollars."

Judge Watkins slammed his gavel on the bench and court was adjourned. The sheriff returned and handcuffed Ouida then escorted her over to the county detention center. Dwanna and Elizabeth followed closely behind.

"Ouida, don't you worry! We have church this evening and will take up an offering to pay your bond! We will get you out of here and back home until the hearing. Do you hear me precious one?"

Ouida wouldn't look back at her as she disappeared into the county lockup.

STOCKPILE

"Tater, Tater! Did you hear? Did you hear!"

"I did Cue! It's so awful! They said it's all her fault that this underground moonshine business has been running so strong in the county. This is the biggest scandal Shepherd, Texas has ever had! Maybe this will be just the thing that really puts us on the map!"

Cueball shook his head and collapsed in the big leather chair in Tater's office.

"Look Cue, I know you and Ouida have been on the outs, but she really will be alright don't ya think?"

"I sure hope so. I just really don't see her being the mastermind behind such a thing. She isn't one to get caught up in this kind of stuff! I know she likes to have a little business on the side now and then but I don't really think she is capable of leading such a big operation as what's been happenin' around here the past few months."

"Well, I heard that Elizabeth Mayhaw from Coldspring is on the case. They say she is the best criminal attorney in the county. I'm sure she will find a loophole to get Ouida back on the streets again."

Cueball shook his head and laid it on the back of his chair, staring at the ceiling for half the morning in disbelief of what had happened.

"What are ya'll doin' lazin' around on the job?" Murphy asked as he entered Tater's office.

"Why Daddy, we didn't hear you drive up."

"Well, darlin', you were definitely focused on something more important than visitors."

"Well, yes we were Daddy. Did you hear about. . ."

"Ouida getting arrested for trafficking moonshine? Yes, I did. Jess called me last night to let me in on everything. He said he still has a gut feeling this isn't all Ouida's doing. He thinks there's someone else who is the ringmaster of this operation and Ouida is just a pawn to throw law enforcement off the trail. He said they are holding her in custody to try to get more information out of her about how she got the hooch, who sold it to her and who else in town she thinks might be distributing it."

"Well, it's a good thing Uncle Jess has that intuition about him. He can always see the full picture although it takes a while for him to put the pieces together."

"I just wanted to drop by and see how my Sunshine and her crew are doin' today. I left some hot glazed Shipley donuts out by the coffee maker for you all. Hope you enjoy!"

Shipley donuts were Tater's favorite. She had been eating them since she was knee high to a grasshopper. Just the thought of that oozing, sugary, fresh yeast dough goodness make her hop out of her chair and head to the break room. Her Daddy headed towards the front door.

"Check ya later ali-Tater!"

"Love you Daddy!"

Tater quickly reached into the Shipley box and stuffed a steamy hot glazed donut into her mouth. Cueball followed right behind her.

Tater walked outside with Cueball and met Patty in the yard as she was waving off one of the delivery drivers.

"You take care of yourself now there Kody. I hope to hear from you when you are able!"

"Able what?"

"Oh nothin' Cue"

Patty pointed towards the road.

"Looks like Mrs. Sanderson's corn delivery lost a bag or two on FM 1127 this mornin'. It was scattered all over the road and blew in here. The crows were out havin' a heyday when I opened up."

"That Mrs. Sanderson raises the best damn hogs this side of the Trinity River if you ask me. You wouldn't know they were raised on the farm unless you asked her yourself. Taste just like the ones my Uncle Jess hunts up in the Piney Woods."

"Yes, they sure do Tater. They are definitely the best in this area. I hear she sells her hogs and ships them all the way to Japan as a delicacy. Woooooo! She must really make a ton of money being in that line of work. Where can we get a piece of that?"

Murphy stepped onto the Feed Store porch and grabbed a Co-Cola out of the box, slid the cap against the porch rail and popped the bottle top off . He sat down in one of the oversized rockers and stretched is lanky legs in front of him.

"Hey Lobo, what you make of this Ouida Lawless stuff?"

"Framed, framed for sure. When did you ever know of Ouida being so smart that she could secretly sell bootleg to just about everyone in town and get away with it. . .much less run the entire operation?"

"You definitely got a point there Lobo. Jess thinks the same thing and he is destined to get to the bottom of this."

"Well, we are all keepin' our ears on, if you know what I mean Murph."

Murphy and Mr. Lobo clinked their Co-Cola bottles together and said "Cheers!"

Later on, Mr. Lobo walked into his house and met Mrs. Carol standin' by the kitchen island lookin' square in his direction.

"What Momma?"

Mr. Lobo flashed a boyish grin at her.

"Did you see this Lobo! There's more stuff goin' on with

that moonshine even with Ouida in the pokey!"

Mr. Lobo took a look at the headline of the East Texas Times which read, "Stockpile of Moonshine Discovered at Local Homeless Pantry."

"Good Lord! This definitely is gettin' to be a problem around here. And, yes Momma, this is not a Ouida level operation!"

Mr. Lobo headed to his office and picked up his CB radio handset to get Sam Green's, aka Veggie Man, attention.

"Breaker breaker 1-9, Veggie Man you copy?"

"10-4 Papa Bear, what's your twenty?"

"Have you seen the paper?"

"I was just lookin' at that Papa Bear."

"I can't believe they been hidin' this stuff over at the homeless shelter. I guess it was the safest place for those traffickers down here."

"Right, I think we can definitely figure this thing out. It's hard to believe this is just sittin' right under our noses when no one can put their finger on it yet. I'm sure Sheriff Jess is havin' a helluva time puttin' the pieces together."

"Most definitely, Papa Bear."

"You still got your cameras up and runnin' by the vegetable stand right?"

"Sure do."

"Well, I think I'm going to put a few up strategically around my lot and keep an eye on things down here in the river bottom. You think I can pick a couple up at Radio Shack?"

"Heck yeah. That's exactly where I got mine. Get the wireless one's so you can spread them around your property without having to drag wires all over the place. Put them in somethin' that isn't noticeable to the normal passerby like I did by using my bird houses."

"Yeah, I think I'll put them in my gourds. No one will ever suspect I have cameras in those. Well, Veggie Man, thank ya much. Will catch ya on the flip side."

"10-4 Papa Bear, I think I might add a couple more around here. We can compare notes in a few days. Over and out."

Mr. Lobo persuaded Mrs. Carol to take a ride into Livingston with him to pick up the cameras from Radio Shack.

Cueball dropped by Sallie Jean's diner after work that afternoon. Sallie Jean was as perky and plump as the day she was born.

"Hi purty girl. You sure do look beautiful in that apron and denim dress!"

Cueball reached over and pushed her curly hair behind her ears. He loved the way she looked and took a moment to breathe her in. She smiled that icebreaker smile of hers.

"Hey honey! What brings you here tonight?"

"I just need my lovin' pumpkin and some of your good

cookin' to soothe my soul after a long hard day."

Cueball laid a kiss on her right cheek.

"Well, honey, just sit down and I'll get you your favorite."

Sallie Jean disappeared into the kitchen and Cueball got up and pulled the local paper off a table next to him. He read the same headline Mrs. Carol had shared with Mr. Lobo earlier that day. Cueball shook his head in amazement and turned to the police blotter to add some local humor to his weary self.

The police blotter is somethin' you find in a small town paper that basically provides the locals with the criminal activity in the county on a case-by-case basis.

Cueball read the blotter out loud to himself.

"Mrs. Evans caught a man relieving himself in the wash sink out in her back yard early Saturday morning and when she screamed, the perpetrator flashed his man parts and went running into the woods behind her property. Local police are still looking for the man.

Mr. Hansen's old coon dog was found flat on his back, feet in the air and snout caught in a mason jar late Sunday afternoon. The dog was out like a light. Mr. Hansen said the jar contained some of that moonshine they been talking about around town. Police politely searched Mr. Hansen's house and helped him grease the jar off the passed out hound's snout. No moonshine was found on his property and the old hound was ultimately unharmed.

Mr. Beverly's old billy goat was found out back of Crazy Jane's house chewing her lady garments off the clothes line. Crazy Jane fired her shotgun off into the air to scare the goat off yet it ricocheted off her gutter and lodged into her backside leaving her screaming for help. Mr. Beverly heard the gunshot, as well as her screams, and called the local police department for assistance."

Sallie Jean heard Cueball laughin' his heart out as she brought his dinner to the table.

"What's so funny honey?"

"Oh this here police blotter will take the pain out of any hard day."

"Oh yeah, the Crazy Jane piece was the best, wasn't it honey?"

Cueball nodded his head yes and immediately placed his attention on the piled high plate of mashed potatoes and chicken fried steak slathered in cream gravy.

That same evenin', Capt. Clyde dropped by to visit with Mrs. Carol and Mr. Lobo. They were sittin' on the porch when Clyde piped up.

"Lobo, you know those UPS trucks we been seein' drivin' up and down here? Well, I have seen the same trucks up and down US 59 between Cleveland and Livingston the past couple of days. I've had to go in both directions to run some errands and found it odd that those same trucks were travelin' up and down the highway. I know it was the same trucks because they have the same 'Share the Road' bumper stickers on the back bumpers. Funny thing is none of the other UPS trucks have bumper stickers on them. I just have a very strange suspicion as to whether they may somehow be tied to this moonshine operation."

"Well, I have my cameras up and am recordin' the comin's and goin's of vehicles down here so maybe we can put our finger on somethin' very soon. Have you noticed any activity down by you early in the mornin' with those trucks drivin' down Robin Lane?"

"Well, come to think of it, they have been makin' deliveries to that old bitch's house next to me. However, I just thought they were deliverin' that work she is doin' billin' for the medical company."

"Well, I think there's more to that than meets the eye Clyde. Do me a favor and see if you can't get more info on when exactly those trucks are landin' at her place."

Clyde went on home about an hour later and decided to make his homestead rituals a bit more observant.

The next morning, Clyde made a point of sitting out on the east side of his porch overlookin' the old bitch's yard just to piss her off . He stepped outside in his boxer shorts, tank and house slippers with a hot thermos of coffee and the daily paper. She looked up from her back garden and glared at him stabbing her hoe into the dirt, turning and stomping back into her house. They did not have a neighborly relationship to say the least.

Rumor has it one day Clyde was out workin' in his yard and went across the street to his adjacent lot to pick up some limbs and garbage when the old hag pulled up. She jumped out of her car screamin' and rantin' and ravin'.

"What the hell you doin' trespassin' on that property? I'm going to call the police and have them arrest you!"

Clyde saluted her with the middle finger of fellowship and went back to workin' on his lot.

She drove back over to her house, picked up the phone and called the police. Thirty minutes later, the local officers showed up and asked Clyde to step over to their vehicle. Of course the old bitch wanted to hear everything so she decided to walk on over and join in the conversation as well.

One of the officers approached Clyde and asked, "Sir, what is your interest in this lot?"

"I tried to tell that woman I own the lot! It's my property. If you look over there, I just had a new septic system installed and it feeds over to the lot my house sits on!"

The officer looked at the woman.

"Ma'am, did he explain this to you before you called?"

"He did not mention a damn word about it officer. And, while we are at it, I will tell you that his fence sits on my property and I want someone out here to give him a restrainin' order until he moves it over to his boundary line."

"That is something you will have to prove through survey and would have to submit it to the judge in Coldspring. The local police department has nothin' to do with meets and bounds. I would highly encourage you to make sure you have your facts straight before you call us again. This time, I'm goin' to let it slide but I am makin' a note of this because next time you will be cited for the trouble."

This was the kind of thing the old woman would do to Clyde and his wife over and over again. Clyde could never figure out why she had it in for him. Either she was just a trouble maker doin' what she could to bully folks down here in the river bottom or she was hidin' somethin' and by causin' such a ruckus it took the spotlight off of her.

As Clyde continued relaxing out on his deck, he noticed one of the UPS trucks pullin' up to the old bitch's place. There was an exchange made out of view of Clyde as her front door was on the other side of her house. However, a few minutes later, a 1970s Toyota four by four drove up to her place and tossed a few boxes into its bed. Next thing Clyde knew, the Toyota was roundin' the corner in front of his house and stopped at the gate to the road leadin' down to the Trinity River sand bar. The driver got out of the truck, unlocked the gate, drove down the road and didn't emerge until approximately a half hour later.

Clyde noticed the boxes in the back of the Toyota were no longer there.

PUNKIN'

Coco sat in the cell next to Ouida and glared at her through her swollen eye. Ouida looked at Coco and spit on the ground in front of her.

"You think you all that you rug muncher?"

"You wish you could have a piece of me?"

"You couldn't handle me Coco bitch."

Ouida looked at Coco again and flipped her the bird. Coco threw some gang sign at her and laid down to take a snooze.

Sheriff Jess appeared on the other side of the cell bars and motioned to Ouida.

"Let's talk."

He unlocked the doors and led Ouida into one of the interrogation rooms and asked her to sit down.

"This may take us a while so you best get comfortable."

"Where the hell is my lawyer?"

"You don't need a lawyer for this Ouida as long as you behave yourself. Now, where shall we start? Oh yes, where in the world did you really get that moonshine Ouida? You first told me you simply left money on the back stoop in a mason jar and the next mornin' you would miraculously find a supply waiting for you. Now, I know that's not the story Ouida and if we can make some headway today, I might have a chat with Judge Watkins to see if we can't get you on home."

Ouida looked at him, looked at the floor and scratched her head.

"Well, let's just say there wasn't that gap between me puttin' the money on the stoop and the hooch miraculously appearin'. All I can truly tell you is that Coon-Ass Joe was the one drivin' that mess over to my icehouse. He said he was meetin' somebody each mornin' over at the Slots Shack and gettin' the hooch from him. Said the guy bringin' it was not from these parts. Said he was from Polk County but chose San Jacinto County to be his distribution center on account it was easier to move this stuff around with the reduced law enforcement out here."

"Now, we are makin' a little headway Ouida. I'm wonderin' if you would be interested in helpin' us find this guy with the intent to give you probation for your role in all of this?"

"Plea damn bargain huh Sheriff?"

Sheriff Jess nodded his head yes.

"Well, then, I'm in."

Sheriff Jess took Ouida back to her cell and thanked her for her help.

Coco looked over at her.

"You took a plea you chicken shit didn't you?"

"You're damn right I did you muther fuckin' dyke!"

"Well, when you get out of here, you better be watchin' your back because I know where you live and I will come pay you a visit."

"I'm not scared a you Coco pussy shit muffer!"

Early the next mornin' Sheriff Jess opened Ouida's cell and brought her into the release area of the station. Dwanna was waitin' for her with a bottle of Dr. Pepper and a jalapeño and egg burrito from Sonic. Ouida was so tired and over this mess that she didn't know what to do. She didn't have the energy to expletive up the place before she left.

"Sheriff, thank you for working things out with me. I 'preciate you."

"I'll call you in a day or so, after you get some rest, and we will talk more then."

Dwanna gently grabbed Ouida by the arm and led her out to her Cadillac. As they buckled up in the car Dwanna looked over at Ouida.

"Darlin', you look terrible. I'm gonna take you to my house, get you all cleaned up and tucked in for a good long slumber."

All Ouida could do in response was break down and cry all the way to Dwanna's house. She didn't want anything to do with her goodness but couldn't resist someone takin' care of her for once in her life.

Dwanna pulled into her driveway, got out of the car and walked to the passenger side and eased Ouida out. She walked her into the house and ran a hot bath for her. Ouida soaked in the tub for over an hour and finally dressed and sat down to supper. Afterwards, she stretched out on the guest bed and was out for the count. Her dreams carried her off to her childhood.

"Daddy!"

"Shut up Ouida Mae or you're next!"

"Daddy! Don't hurt Momma! She didn't do nothin' wrong!"

"Listen here you little piece of fuckin' shit, I told you to stay out of this!"

Suddenly Ouida's face stung and she could taste blood trickling from her nose. She balled her fists up and began pounding on her Daddy's back. Her brother, Wayne Jr., sat wailing in the corner.

"Leave him alone Ouida! He told you to stay out of it!"

Ouida's daddy grabbed her by the hair and her brother by his arm and dragged them into the back bedroom locking the door.

Ouida put her ear to the door.

"Wayne! I didn't do anything! I don't know why you think I did! I've been here all day with the children!"

"Shut up you sorry ass bitch! You mother fuckin' have to pay for the goddamn shit trouble you got me into!"

Ouida heard her mother hit the ground and a gasp of air come from her mouth. Her daddy flung the bedroom door open walking over to Ouida. He had a Colt .38 in his hand. Grabbing Ouida's hair she reflexively opened her mouth to cry. He stuck the barrel of the gun in her mouth. She could taste the metal and began to sob louder.

"You tell anyone about this today, Ouida Mae, I'll first blow your mother fuckin' head off and then I'll take that brother of yours and blow his goddamn head off after that. You understand me you illegitimate piece of shit?"

Ouida nodded her head yes as tears streamed down her face. Wayne continued to sob in the corner and it was evident he soiled himself out of fear. Her daddy slammed the bedroom door and locked it behind him. Ouida could hear his footsteps wandering across the house, keys jingled and the door slammed. The old 1948 Ford muscled out of the driveway and headed down the road.

No one in the little town of Punkin knew the torment Ouida and her brother endured until the night her daddy killed their momma. He locked the children in the house and had not returned from an evenin' of drinkin'. While they were left alone in their home, a fire broke out due to faulty electrical wiring from the percolator plugged into the kitchen wall. A neighbor noticed smoke coming from the window and called 911. The volunteer fire department raced over to put out the blaze of what they thought was an abandoned shack until they heard Ouida and her brother screamin' from inside. The firefighters busted down the door of the house and carried the two kids outside. They immediately made a call to Child Protective Services who sent out Ms. Annette, their savin' grace.

A while later, Ms. Annette walked up to the children. Ouida looked up at the towering woman and felt she was meeting a princess. Her long hair caressed Ouida's face as she reached down to scoop her up. Ouida peered into her eyes.

"Are you a princess?"

"No, Ouida, but you sure are!"

With Ouida in her arms, she knelt down beside Wayne and pulled him close to her as well. She quickly turned the children away from the house as the coroner wheeled a stretcher carrying their charred momma's remains to an ambulance.

"Children, we are going to get you out of here and placed somewhere folks are going to love and protect you."

"Where's momma?" questioned Ouida.

"Where's momma!" cried Wayne.

"Children, let's get you cleaned up and get a good meal in your bellies. Then, we will talk about your sweet momma ."

Ms. Annette took the kids home with her that evening. After they bathed and were fed they near fell asleep at the table. Ms. Annette carried them to her spare bedroom, tucked them in and sang them to sleep.

The next morning, Ouida and Wayne showed up at the breakfast table and commenced to inhale a plate of biscuits and gravy. Ouida looked up at Ms. Annette.

"Is our Momma gone Ms. Annette?"

Ms. Annette turned towards the children, sat down at the table and grabbed both their hands.

"Yes, children, your momma took a severe beating and they believe she died even before the fire broke out in your house yesterday."

Wayne looked at Ms. Annette, tears welling in his eyes.

"What about Daddy?"

"Your Daddy was picked up by the police when he had a little accident in his truck. The police learned of his address while questioning him and determined he possibly was the one responsible for your momma's dying and you two being locked in the house."

Ouida and Wayne burst into tears. Ms. Annette could tell the tears were for the loss of their momma mixed with a relief their daddy couldn't get to them any longer.

"Don't you worry about that daddy of yours, the officers have him in a place he will never hurt anyone again."

Over the next few weeks, CPS could not find a home that would accept Ouida and her brother together. Ouida ended up with a family down in Shepherd and her brother was sent up to northeast Texas to live with another family in Athens. Ouida never heard from her brother after that. She was broken hearted losing the only friend she ever had.

The Plan

Ouida's eyes opened twelve hours later to the smell of hot coffee and fresh cinnamon buns. She tidied herself up and walked down the hallway to Dwanna's kitchen.

"Well, good mornin' Sunshine! How you feelin'?"

Dwanna motioned to her to take a seat.

"Thank you for pickin' me up and havin' me stay here last night Dwanna."

Ouida began to cry.

Dwanna sat down next to her and held her hand.

"Precious One, everything's going to be all right."

Ouida burst out in tears again unsure of what the future was goin' to hold for her.

There was a knock on the door and Sheriff Jess stepped in.

"Good mornin' Dwanna. It sure does smell good in here. Mornin' Ouida, did you get some rest?"

Ouida nodded her head yes and motioned for him to sit at the kitchen table with them.

"I have a proposal for you this mornin' Ouida. Let's get started on our game plan and see if we can't get to the bottom of this once and for all. I hope you are ready Ouida because we are goin' to be mighty busy the next few days."

Ouida dried her eyes and leaned forward indicating she was ready to talk through his strategy.

"Ouida, I have contacted the FBI and ATF who are sending agents down here to work this investigation with us."

"With us Sheriff?"

"Yes, Ouida, they are going to work with us and get to the bottom of who is runnin' this moonshine operation."

"Am I gonna have to wear a wire Sheriff?"

"No, nothin' like that Ouida. There will be some investigative action going on all the same."

"Well, thank the damn Lard, I'm too fuckin' sophisticated to have to do somethin' like that."

The sheriff looked over at Dwanna and smiled.

"That's our Ouida," replied Dwanna. "Sheriff, why are both the FBI and ATF involved?"

"Dwanna, this is kind of a double header here with the investigation, being it's moonshine and all. The operation falls under the 'A' for alcohol and the FBI is getting involved because this is a Federal offense."

"Ah, so like one of those sting operations I seen on that CSI show?" asked Ouida.

"That's right Ouida, you can call it that."

"Well, this sounds like fun!"

"Well, Ouida, we have to keep up appearances and make it look like we are going about business as usual. Nothing that would tip anyone off the wiser."

"How in the world is this going to look like business as usual Sheriff with them snooping around town?"

"Dwanna, I'm glad you asked, we are going to take advantage of the Camp Meeting crowd headed to town and ensure they blend in during this next week."

Dwanna was excited about the plan and tickled pink that folks would think these out-of-towners would be part of their congregation.

"Dwanna, there is one thing I would like to ask you."

"Sure Sheriff, anything to help."

"We would like to use your house here as the base camp. All you need to do is provide them with a place to sleep, a table to work out their strategy and provide enough coffee and baked goods to keep them sugared up throughout the investigation."

"Sheriff, I can certainly do that. I'm glad to help out any way I can. The Lord didn't put me on this earth to sit around and do nothin'."

The Holy Rollers were headin' into town that Friday afternoon to get ready for the big Camp Meetin' Kickoff at the Tabernacle. The town hadn't seen that much hair and long skirts in no tellin' how long. Murphy and Mr. Lobo were sittin' on the feed store porch and couldn't believe the big revival bus that drove down the town center followed by what seemed to be a thousand cars stuffed with tongue talkers.

"Well, hell Murph! I know where I'm steerin' clear of this weekend! Maybe Momma and I should head on down to Bolivar and do some fishin' until they all rapture out of here."

"I'm right behind you two Lobo."

The Tabernacle parkin' lot was overflowin'. They had set up an additional tent outside to hold the extra guests that wouldn't fit into the main sanctuary. There were guest preachers comin' from all over East Texas as this was the first time The Tabernacle held such an event. It was The Tabernacle's 100th year anniversary and definitely a time for some good old fashioned Camp Meetin' celebrations. The town businesses were thrilled as peaches there would be such an onslaught of Bible beaters durin' the weekend. Anytime a big event was held nearby they would get the spillover in commerce. This time was different because they were stayin' right in their own backyard. Every diner, cafe and drive-through was ready and waitin' to feed the hungry crowd. Every gift shop was spruced up and ready to get their hands into the pocketbooks of those preachers' wives. Even JT's, the local gas station/convenience store, was ready for the influx with a tanker standin' by with additional fuel for the vehicles in town.

Late Friday afternoon, Dwanna heard a knock at her door. Four individuals stood flashing their credentials indicating they were the agents Sheriff Jess spoke of. One of the agents was a female who wore a black skirt suit and heels. Her hair flowed freely down her back and she hadn't put on a lick of makeup that day. Someone could have mistaken her for Dwanna's spiritual sister. The other three males wore black suits, hair cut close to their heads and flashed the shiniest grins Dwanna had ever seen.

"Ms. Crabtree, I'm Agent Weems. I'm the lead ATF agent in charge of this investigation."

"Glad to meet you ma'am."

"I'm Agent Thompson working together with Agent Weems. Agents Walters and Horton are part of the FBI and are collaborating with us in this investigation. We are thankful for your hospitality and will try not to be underfoot too much while we are here."

"Let me show you your rooms. I'm sure you want to get out of those suits and freshen up."

Dwanna took them to their rooms and showed them where the guest bathroom was located. They all disappeared for a few minutes into the back of the house and emerged shortly thereafter in jeans, t-shirts, cowboy boots and ball caps. Even Agent Weems looked like one of the boys with the exception of a pony tail hanging out the back of her cap.

"Looks like you all are ready for business."

"Yes, ma'am, we are headed to Ouida's icehouse to get the lay of the land and a feel for the local nightlife."

"Well, you definitely will get a feel for it there. It's right about happy hour now so the place should be packed."

Dwanna picked up the phone.

"Hey sweetness, your guests are on their way."

"Thanks for the damn warnin'. It's fuckin' busy here and I don't got no time for this right now!"

Ouida hung up the phone and looked over at Coon-Ass Joe.

"Joe, how did things fare while I was away?"

"Oh, fine. Yah help done did a great job keepin' erthing in erder whiles you wuz gone."

Coon-Ass Joe laid his head down on the bar. A second later, he popped his head back up startling Ouida.

"Oh yah, an I put some o' dat shipment in dat dare back storge arah just like you tolt me."

"Oh shit!"

About that time Sheriff Jess stepped in and walked over to the bar.

"Welcome back Ouida. I hope you are doin' well and no feelings hurt?"

"No feelin's hurt Sheriff. Can you come over here, I need to tell you somethin'."

Ouida met the Sheriff at the far end of the bar and leaned over to him.

"On account I'm not gunna hide anything from you, you

need to know that Joe brought me a shipment while I was away and it's sittin' in the back stockroom."

"Thank you Ouida, I'll make note of that and let our visitors know as well. I appreciate your honesty. Tell me you won't touch any of it?"

Ouida shook her head no and gave him a wink.

"Well, gotta go, hope you have a productive night tonight Ouida. Bye, Joe."

Coon-Ass Joe looked over at him and waved a one-finger wave. Gomer gave up a friendly bark.

The crowd that night was thick at the icehouse. Some had snuck in from the Camp Meetin'. Ouida found out from Dwanna, later, that they were known as "Backsliders." Basically men or women who just did their duty by driving their spouses up to the Camp Meeting then ditching them for a trip over to the bar. These were the kind of folks their religious spouses hung onto thinkin' one day they would "turn from their evil ways." However, by the looks of them and the amount of booze they were slammin' back told Ouida otherwise. These folks were definitely not in any hurry to run back to their Jesus.

Coon-Ass Joe looked up at Ouida from the bar.

"You goin' to dat Camp Meetin' tomorrah?"

"Hell no! I have no fuckin' intention of gettin' myself all caught up in that judgmental bullshit! I don't have a judgmental bone in my body but them Holy Rollers are the worst!"

"Well, I dunt tink I be showin' up dare needer."

Three guys and a gal stepped into the smoke-filled icehouse and walked up to the bar.

"Two Cokes and a Sprite highball please."

The icehouse served beer as well as highballs for those bringin' in their own liquor. The four agents had a bottle of Jack Black that was filled with some amber colored liquor posin' as whiskey. They paid for the highballs and made their way to a corner table.

Coon-Ass Joe looked at Ouida.

"By de way Ouida, I are gone to go pick up anuder round fer ya tomarrah. Will dat work?"

"Sure, Joe. That will be just fine."

She looked over at the four sittin' in the corner and walked over to the table with another round of highballs.

"This one's on me yunguns. I'm Ouida, the owner of this here establishment. I've got someone pickin' me up some more highballs tomorrow mornin'."

Ouida gave them a big wink and laid a beverage napkin on the table. The napkin was scribbled with the words "Pickup at Slots Shack 9am tomorrow. Early bird gamblin' hour. Old Joe at bar making run."

"Thank you Ms. Ouida, this was mighty fine of you to bring us a round."

Agent Weems let out a burp catching Ouida by surprise for once in her life.

UNDERCOVER

The Slots Shack parking lot was flooded with cars early the next morning. Agents Walters and Horton were inside blending with the crowd of gamblers. They witnessed Coon-Ass Joe heading in with Gomer. He pulled a couple of one-armed bandits. Jiles, the Slots Shack owner, came around the corner and nodded hello to Coon-Ass Joe indicating he had loaded a supply of moonshine into his car. Joe got up, walked over to Jiles, shook his hand all the while exchanging a wad of cash within the shake. Agents Walters and Horton witnessed the transaction.

Agents Weems and Thompson were over at the antique furniture store next door running surveillance. They were posing as husband and wife figuring they would probably be doing a lot of surveillance from the store over the next couple of days. Agent Thompson flashed a smile at Agent Weems.

"Honey, I really like this table here. Do you think this will fit into the car or are we goin' to have to get Bubba to help us pick it up?"

The old woman running the shop smiled at them both.

"Well, I don't think it will fit in the car. Let me give Bubba a call."

They continued to browse the store for another hour as the agents at the Slots Shack continued their surveillance on the inside. Agent Weems made the call, mumbled some jibber and hung up.

"Honey, Bubba's not gonna make it over here today. We are gonna have to come back."

Agent Thompson walked over to the shop owner.

"Thank you ma'am. You have a very nice shop here. We will be back tomorrow."

The agents decided to head back to Dwanna's for supper and a nap before they hit the night beat.

Dwanna was waiting for them when they arrived. She had a fresh pot of coffee on and a casserole in the oven. It was nice having company for a change even if it was the Feds.

"Hey y'all, how about a hot cup of coffee? I'm sure you all could use a little rest as well. I don't think you have slept since you got here. I've turned down the twin beds in the back guest room, opened the sleeper sofa in the office and dressed the couch up over there. I'll make sure everything stays nice and quiet around here. Now, sit yourselves down and get some nourishment in those stomachs of yours. I'm sure you have a long night ahead of you."

"Well, thank you Ms. Dwanna. We can't thank you enough for your hospitality and want you to know that you are doin' a tremendous service to law enforcement and the United States of America."

"Well, I'm glad to help. Now once y'all lie down, I'll be headed to the Camp Meetin' for the evenin'. Here's a key so you can let yourself in and out as you please. If you need anything, you just feel free to poke around."

The agents refueled and took turns taking a couple hours snooze. A few hours later they began to strategize the evening's plan. They decided that two of them would run surveillance from retired officer James' parking area on the corner of FM 1127 and US 59. James was a former officer at the Shepherd substation and Sheriff Jess asked him to allow the agents to park their vehicle in his drive to monitor the Slots Shack. Agents Weems and Thompson parked outside the antique store and pretended they were two lovers just smooching it up if someone drove by.

The late night surveillance proved fruitless. The Slots Shack closed at 11pm and the parking area was deader than a doornail for the rest of the night. Agents Weems and Thompson headed back to Dwanna's to fill up their thermos' with hot fresh coffee. They dropped a thermos by the other agents vehicle and returned to the antique shop parking lot kicking off the early dawn shift. Just before daybreak a UPS delivery truck drove up behind the Slots Shack. Right after that, Jiles drove up to the front of the Slots Shack in his dark brown 1960 El Camino accented with yellow stripes and Cragar mag wheels. He unlocked the door and went inside. Agents Weems and Thompson noticed the back door had opened when the motion lights went off out behind the building. They radioed the others.

"We have some activity over here. Get ready to follow this guy out. We believe he just delivered a load to the Slots Shack."

"We've got the motor warmed up and are ready as soon as we see him exit the property."

"The description of the vehicle and plates are as follows, appears to be a brown UPS delivery truck Texas license plates MTR777."

They ran the vehicle plates which listed a Kody Nash out of Cleveland, Texas as owner. Thirty minutes later the brown delivery truck was leaving the property headed south on US 59. Agents Walters and Horton exited the parking lot, crossed the highway and headed south behind the van. The other two agents decided to go pay old Jiles a visit. They stepped in through the back door only to find Jiles stacking 30 cases of moonshine in his storage room. Jiles looked up in surprise and dropped a case which promptly shattered all over the place. The two agents introduced themselves.

"Mr. Jiles, I'm Agent Weems and this is Agent Thompson from the Houston bureau of the ATF. We are here to arrest you for possession and trafficking of moonshine."

Mr. Jiles looked at the two stunned, turned around and made a b-line for the front door. Agent Weems ran after him while Agent Thompson headed out the back door and around to the front. Jiles had already hopped into his El Camino and was headed out of the drive. Agents Weems and Thompson hopped into their car and followed Jiles north on US 59. They had no trouble staying on the tail of Jiles' El Camino. They figured it wouldn't take long for him to pull over and give up knowing that he couldn't outrun them.

Sheriff Jess received a call about the chase and headed out to catch up with them. Jiles' El Camino blew a tire right in front of the Goodrich Truck Stop. He pulled off the road and was promptly greeted by Agent Weems at his car door.

"Get out of the car with your hands up Mr. Jiles."

Jiles got out of the car with his hands raised. Agent Weems spun him around to face the car and handcuffed his arms behind him. Agent Weems read Jiles his rights. Sheriff Jess walked up.

"Jiles, you know better than this."

Jiles looked at the sheriff.

"You know I'll be up and runnin' again in about a month. No sweat off my back Sheriff."

Agent Thompson smiled at Jiles.

"Mr. Jiles, where we are taking you, you won't be coming back here for a long while."

Agent Weems introduced herself as Agent Kelly Weems

and her partner as Agent Butch Thompson of the Houston Division of the ATF and loaded Jiles into their vehicle and headed down to Houston to place him in custody.

Meanwhile Agent Walters and his partner continued to discreetly follow the brown delivery truck south on US 59. The UPS truck's blinker kicked on and the driver turned right down the side street parallel to McMann's supermarket. Agent Walters and his partner parked across the street at the gas station and watched the activity. The brown truck backed up to the loading dock of the super market. The door to the loading dock swung open and a young woman appeared and helped offload ten cases of the moonshine. She handed the driver an envelope, kissed him on the cheek and waved goodbye. The driver then headed further down the street and hung a left onto Byrd Avenue. He drove past the Justice of the Peace's office, continued through the traffic signal and hung a right into the Post Office parking lot. Agent Walters and his partner drove around the corner and parked next to the Masonic Lodge providing them a clear view of the Post Office loading zone. Again, the driver backed into the receiving area of the Post Office and a woman exited the Post Office back door with a dolly. She offloaded five cases of moonshine, passed a small Priority Mail box to the driver and returned inside. The driver set out to make another stop at the auto parts store on Texas 150. He backed up to the front door where the owner met him outside. Agent Walters and his partner stepped around the driver's side of the delivery truck.

"Hands up, you both are under arrest for trafficking and distributing moonshine."

Agent Walters and his partner promptly handcuffed the two men and placed them in their car. Walters bent down to speak to the two men seated in the back of the car.

"I'm Agent Frank Walters and this is Agent Jackson Horton with the Houston division of the FBI. We have another unit coming to apprehend your delivery truck Mr. Nash and we will be taking you both into Houston for questioning. You have the right to remain silent, understand that anything you say will be used against you in a court of law, you have the right to an attorney and to have them present during questioning and if you cannot afford an attorney, the court will appoint one for you. Do you understand?"

Both of the men nodded their heads in agreement and didn't say another word.

Shortly thereafter Sheriff Jess and his officers visited McMann's and the Post Office and arrested the women who accepted the deliveries as well as confiscated the moonshine they had received from the driver.

"Breaker breaker 1-9, you copy Papa Bear?"

"Ten Four Veggie Man, what's your twenty?"

"Looks like we just had us a sting down here in Shepherd

this mornin'."

"Yeeee Hawwwww! Nothin' like a rabble rousin' to get everything goin' this fine day Veggie Man!"

"Twenty that. Evidently the FBI is now on this moonshine case and is in cahoots with Sheriff Jess. They busted old Jiles this mornin' and shut his business down. In addition to that, another couple of agents followed the guy makin' the delivery and caught him droppin' off at McMann's, the Post Office and Mike's Auto Supply over there across from JT's. So not only did they arrest the delivery driver, they also arrested the folks at the businesses who took the deliveries. Guess what, that vehicle the trafficker was drivin' looked like a brown UPS delivery truck Papa Bear!"

"Tax dollars definitely workin' for us today Veggie Man."

Ring ring, ring ring. Tater picked up her phone.

"Hello love of my life!"

"Hey Daddy, how are you?"

"I'm fine Tater Bug, just wanted you to know your Uncle Jess has been working with the FBI on the moonshine case and made a pretty big bust this morning in town."

"Well, I'll be. Let me know the details once you hear more Daddy. Thanks for the call, love you!"

Tater walked out to the yard to check on things. She couldn't believe how well everything was moving along with the operation and how much business had grown over the past few months. It was the best thing she ever did and she was so grateful for the support and backing to make sure the business grew. In addition, she couldn't have asked for a better crew than Cueball, Patty, Marvin and the truck drivers.

Camp Meeting

Ouida dropped by Dwanna's for coffee the next morning on her way to work. Dwanna, as usual, had a fresh baked something ready to tear into.

"Dwanna, it looks like the agents are gone for now."

"Yes, Ouida, they evidently had enough information and folks in custody that they could continue their investigation from the home office in Houston. Apparently, however, they have only broken the chain of one of the delivery drivers that was movin' that moonshine around our area. He isn't the only one distributin' down here. The worst thing is they haven't found out who is makin' the stuff and that's where Sheriff Jess and the Feds want to get to the bottom of it."

"Well, I'm not carryin' it in my shop any longer. One, because I'm done with run-ins with the law and two, there's no one buyin' it on our end of town. Everyone is too darn scared to take any of that stuff on."

Mr. Lobo and Murphy were at their usual morning spot on the front of the Feed Store porch solving the world's problems when Sheriff Jess walked up.

"Hey boys! Want to sit a spell with you two if you don't

mind."

Murph motioned him over to an empty rockin' chair.

"Well, sure Jess. Have a seat and take a load off."

Mr. Lobo scratched his beard and looked at Jess questioningly.

"So what's botherin' you today Jess? Anything we can help you with?"

"Well, you know that we had that big bust about a week ago. Broke a link in the chain of this entire moonshine business. The only problem is we have another distributor out there and we haven't figured out who the producer is yet. If you guys would just keep your eyes and ears open for me, I would appreciate it."

"Sure thing, anything for you brother."

"Hey Jess. I might have somethin' interestin' for you to look at back at the house. How about droppin' by in the next day or so?"

"Tomorrow night good Lobo?"

"That'll be fine."

Ouida and Dwanna were swapping gossip at Dwanna's dinner table when a revelation came upon Dwanna.

"Ouida!"

"Whaaaat?"

"Wouldn't you like to go to one of the services over at the

Camp Meeting today? There will be some mighty fine handsome men attending services."

"Now Dwanna, why would I be interested in goin' to some damn Camp Meetin'?"

"Come on Ouida, just join me this one time and I'll never ask you again. Pretty please with sugar on top?"

"Well, I guess I could go for the first meetin'. I'm goin' like this though Dwanna cuz I got to get to the icehouse before the evenin' shift kicks off as it's goin' to be a busy night."

Ouida was dressed in her usual jeans, flip flops and tank top. Dwanna persuaded her to throw one of her blue jean shirts on over the tank top as "it would be cold in the Tabernacle."

The noon service had already begun. Dwanna rushed Ouida into an empty pew end near the center of the tabernacle. The room swelled with the boom of a gospel choir bringin' home the old favorites. Ouida nearly jumped out of her seat as the choir rang out.

"Jesus, Jesus, Jeeeesusssss that's the sweetest name I know."

Dwanna looked at Ouida, mouthing the words to her and smiling all the way through the verse. Dwanna threw her hands up into the air as the choir blurted out.

"Have a little talk with Jesussss, tell him all about your troublesssss."

This got the crowd up on its feet. Suddenly Dwanna and a few others stepped into the aisle and started spinning round and round like they had one too many. Ouida couldn't believe the sight, she hadn't seen anything like it in her life and sat in the pew holding back the laughter that was building inside. Dwanna returned to her seat and the final song kicked off.

"What can wash away my sin? Nothin' but the blood of Jeeeeesussss. . .Oh! precious issss the flooooowwwww. . ."

Dwanna was singin' at the top of her voice and grabbed Ouida to stand up.

"Don't you just feel the power in here today Ouida?"

"What fuckin' power?"

"It's the love of Jesus Ouida Mae! He's loving all over us right now!"

"Dwanna, I don't feel anything other than a bunch of screamers jibber jabbin' some kind of shit I don't even understand!"

"REPENT AND BE BAPTIZED EVERY ONE OF YOU!" The preacher screamed from the pulpit.

Ouida jumped about two feet off the ground, spun on her heels and ran out the front door of the church building clueless as to why the hell that guy had to scream so loud in a place of worship. Dwanna ran after her stopping her in the parking lot.

"Precious One! What happened?"

"I am not goin' back into that place Dwanna! I don't have

anything against your people but those motherfuckers are crazy in there!"

"That's ok honey. I'm just glad you came with me today. I'm goin' back inside and will give you a call later, ok?"

Ouida nodded her head yes, jumped into her newly acquired red Ford F150 and sped down US 59 to the icehouse.

Ouida ran into the icehouse, sat next to Coon-Ass Joe, pulled out her flask of Jack Black and threw the entire thing back. Coon-Ass Joe looked at her.

"Damn Ouida! What da hell dun hap'nd to ya?"

"I'll tell you what the fuck happened to me Joe. That damn Dwanna, bless her heart she means well, she conned me into goin' to the midday Camp Meetin' with her. I get in there and they start singin' songs about a Chocolate Jesus and I look around and there ain't one black person in the room!"

"What da hell is uh Chocolate Jeezuz?"

"Then, Dwanna starts twirlin' around like them people overseas called the Whirlin' Derbies. I saw them on that Discover channel we got on cable. They were just spinnin' and spinnin' and I couldn't believe not a one of them fell over or puked or somethin'! And that's not all, suddenly the preacher gets up in front and starts yellin' at everyone. I almost shit my britches because it just came out of nowhere and all I could do was run the fuck out of there!"

"So ya got into da middle of one of dem holy rollin' shoutin' matches Ouida! Did you get the 'quickenin' while you wuz dar?"

"Quickenin'? First, I damn don't know what the hell the quickenin' is but I will tell you those sons-a-bitches were jibber jabberin' some kind of stuff that sounded like 'who stole ah my Honda, see me tie my bowtie'! I thought they had all gone behind the damn Tabernacle and drank some of that communion wine before service started or somethin'. You will NEVER find me in that place again!"

The next evening Sheriff Jess brought his brother Murphy over to Mr. Lobo's house. Sam Green, aka Veggie Man, was there as well.

"Looks like we are having us a party tonight."

"Well, you would think so wouldn't you Jess? Come on in here to the livin' room and sit down. Sam and I have some home grown movies we would like to show you."

Sheriff Jess and Murphy both looked a bit puzzled but sat down anyway. Mr. Lobo flipped the TV on and put a disc into the DVD player. On the screen images displayed two UPS delivery trucks. Both of them were headed back and forth up and down US 59 regularly during the early morning and late evening hours which Sam had caught from his birdhouse cams. Other images showed the same trucks driving up and down Jesse

Lane in front of Mr. Lobo's house at similar intervals as well.

"Looks like these trucks are makin' an awful lot of deliveries down there off Robin Lane. Sam and I just thought it odd that these two UPS trucks were makin' all these additional trips even though it was after the holidays. We usually only have one UPS driver and she's our regular. We asked her about the other trucks and she said there weren't any other UPS trucks deliverin' down here on a regular basis."

Sheriff Jess looked bewildered and couldn't understand why there were so many UPS trucks down in the river bottom.

"Lobo, may I have a copy of that DVD?"

"Got one ready for you right here."

Mr. Lobo handed Sheriff Jess a copy.

"I'll provide it to the agents and see if they can make any sense of the information here. Lobo, you wouldn't mind them dropping by with more questions would you?"

"Not at all Jess, always glad to help."

Monday morning came around and the agents arrived at Mr. Lobo's house. Mr. Lobo was out on his back porch with Mrs. Carol drinking a cup of coffee and saw them pull into the driveway. He stepped out front to greet them.

"Good mornin' yunguns. Looks like you are ready to go to work with the way you are dressed today."

"Good morning Mr. Lobo. Thought we might ask some

questions, do some surveillance and perhaps help you with a few chores around here today."

"You all are definitely playing the part today, aren't you?"

"Mr. Lobo, I'm Agent Weems."

Agent Weems extended her hand to shake Mr. Lobo's. All of the other agents introduced themselves and greeted him as well.

"You remind me of one of my daughters Agent Weems. What you all need to be aware of around here is I have a knack for giving everyone nicknames. So, Agent Weems, I think I'll call you Short Britches since we don't want to let on that you all are part of this investigation."

Mr. Lobo chuckled and motioned everyone to come on into the house.

The agents sat at the kitchen breakfast bar with Mrs. Carol and Mr. Lobo and talked through their game plan. They anticipated helping Mr. Lobo with his carport throughout the week and stay overnight each night so they could run surveillance out of their home. They brought some fancy recording equipment with them and were able to hook up to Mr. Lobo's gourd cams. They positioned a couple of other cameras out in the yard to capture additional footage of the vehicles driving up and down the street.

The agents and Mr. Lobo headed outside and got to work on the carport. The guys helped him set the posts in the concrete and stabilize them so they could put the roof on the next morning. Agent Weems was working on the roof framing and preparing the Mueller roofing so it would be ready to be installed the next day. They laid off around five that afternoon and sat on the back porch with Mrs. Carol. She and Mr. Lobo were having an adult beverage and the agents opted on having iced tea. Suddenly, one of the UPS trucks came around the corner and headed to Robin Lane. The agents assured Mr. Lobo and Mrs. Carol they were capturing this on tape back in the office and they didn't have to get up to do anything. They apparently didn't want to arouse suspicion. About twenty minutes later, another truck headed down the same direction. They sat and waited and twenty minutes later the first truck was headed out of the neighborhood with the other one following close behind.

"How often does this happen Mr. Lobo?"

"Well, let's see. Momma, wouldn't you say this happens about every other day at this time durin' the week as well as in the mornin'?"

Mrs. Carol nodded her head in agreement.

"That seems to line up with the frequency of deliveries in town as well so they definitely have themselves a well laid out itinerary around here," replied Agent Weems.

Mrs. Carol headed inside and told everyone to get up and come have some dinner before it got too late. She prepared a huge spread of her famous homemade green chicken enchiladas and pinto beans. She motioned everyone to grab a plate and serve themselves. The agents did not hesitate heading straight over to the buffet and making themselves at home.

Following dinner, Agents Weems and Thompson decided to take a ride in their Toyota Tacoma and drive down towards Robin Lane. They were gone for a couple of hours and radioed back to the rest of the guys at Mr. Lobo's house to keep them posted on observations. They hadn't really come up with much as it seemed nice and quiet down on that end. That's when Mr. Lobo had an idea.

"My buddy Clyde has a house in good view of Robin Lane and he would be fine with you hanging out there for additional surveillance."

"Would Clyde have any concerns with us coming by in the morning?" asked Agent Walters.

Mr. Lobo gave Clyde a call.

"Hey Clyde, these agents down here at my place would like to stake out Robin Lane from your porch in the mornin'. Do you mind?"

"Hell no Lobo, I don't mind at all. Tell them to come by around seven a.m. I'll have a fresh pot of coffee waiting for them."

Everyone decided to call it a night and get some shuteye.

The next morning Agents Walters and Horton headed down to Clyde's for a visit. They were sitting on the porch drinking coffee when they noticed the neighbor next door staring right back at them from her back porch.

"Don't mind that old bitch. She's the nosiest troublemaker in our neighborhood. I just ignore her and keep enjoyin' the view."

Clyde promptly stood up, looked over in her direction and promptly shot her the bird. She got up from her rocker and stomped back into her house slamming the screen door behind her. Shortly after that, one of the UPS trucks pulled up in front of the old woman's house and punched in a gate code that allowed them to pull into her drive.

"That old bat works for a medical billing company and gets deliveries a couple of times a week. However, those trucks have been pulling in fairly regularly. They drop a delivery off in the morning and usually one or two more in the evenings," explained Clyde.

The agents didn't have a good view of what was being delivered but suspected she was getting a fair amount of inventory due to the driver being there for a good fifteen minutes. The delivery driver left her property. About ten minutes later a couple of vehicles pulled into her driveway. One was an old 1960s VW Bus that had certainly seen better days. It was splotched in multi colors of paint, a big daisy plastered on the back driver's side, dark tinted windows and rusted wheels that gave it a vintage appearance. The other vehicle was a bright yellow Chevy S-10 pickup with a camper on the back. They remained for ten minutes and then headed back towards town.

"Agent Thompson," radioed Agent Horton.

"Thompson here."

"You and Agent Weems hop in your vehicle and wait for a Chevy S-10 pickup or VW Bus to drive by and tail them. We are sticking around here for a few minutes."

Shortly thereafter, a blue Jeep Wrangler four-by-four drove up and parked in the old woman's driveway. A man got out, knocked on the door and she let him in. A few minutes later, the truck sped off. Clyde noticed it heading over to the Trinity River Road gate about a block from his front porch. The driver got out of the truck and unlocked the gate. He got back in the vehicle and sped down through the open gate.

Clyde pointed towards the gate saying, "That road leads down to the Trinity River sandbar where all the locals hang out. You could call it our neighborhood beach."

Agent Horton radioed for additional backup from a couple of ATF agents positioned at Mount Moriah church off FM 1127 to go check on the blue Jeep down on the sandbar.

Meanwhile, back at Mr. Lobo's house, Agents Weems and Thompson loaded up into their vehicle and along came the VW Bus. The Chevy had taken a different route out of the neighborhood as it was nowhere to be seen. The agents discreetly tailed the VW bus as it headed towards US 59 on FM 1127. The VW bus first stopped at the Lunch Shack on Lilly Hill and dropped off a case. The woman running the place passed him an envelope right about the time the agents drove by. Agents Weems and Thompson continued on down the road and pulled into the Texas Tea, LLC parking lot and took out a map to make it look like they were checking directions.

"Who is that parked out front Cue?"

"No clue, Patty."

The two were indulging themselves in a Shipley sausage and jalapeño kolache. Patty walked over to the end of the yard towards the street to see if she could help them with anything and about that time Agent Weems shifted into gear and drove off. Patty turned and headed back to the porch where Tater and Cueball were sitting.

"More corn spilled all over the road again. What is going on with that delivery driver heading to the pig farm?"

Patty looked at Tater and shrugged her shoulders.

"Patty, you would think we just had a harvest next door over there in the field! If these damn crows don't stop coming around here, I'm going to have to call it open season on their asses."

The VW bus turned north on US 59 and passed the agents

who were waiting at the Slots Shack parking lot. They pulled out of the lot tailing them. The VW bus driver made another stop at the recycling center. As he was dropping off the moonshine, Agents Thompson and Weems met him and the recycling center manager in the front office.

"Hands up, you are both under arrest for trafficking and distributing moonshine."

They both threw their hands up and the agents promptly handcuffed them without a scuffle. The agents introduced themselves, read them their rights and headed on back to Houston with the two.

Agents Horton and Walters decided to go pay the old woman a visit. "Rat-a-tat-tat" Agent Walters knocked on her front door then stepped to the side of the entrance.

"I don't know who the hell gave you the idea you could trespass on my property, but consider yourself warned!"

The agents jumped off the porch when they heard what they thought was her pump a shotgun. She pulled the trigger and a spray of shot shell blew through her front door missing the agents. Walters ran around to the back ot the house and Horton remained at the base of the porch.

"This is Agent Horton with the FBI," he shouted, "Come out with your hands up!"

Another round exploded through the front door.

Afterwards both Agent Walters and the old woman came flying out the shredded entry way. Walters held her face down on the deck, handcuffing her. He turned her over to face him.

"Now that we've got your attention, ma'am, we are going to take you into town for questioning."

"Fuck you!"

The woman spit directly in Agent Walters' face.

Clyde was enjoying the events of the morning out on his porch as he noticed the ATF agents passing through the gate leading down to the Trinity River sandbar. The drive was a muddy potholed mess. It took them about fifteen minutes to travel down a quarter mile road. As they eased off the main road onto the sandbar, they spotted the blue Jeep. The driver had backed it up to the water's edge where a flat bottom fishing boat had come ashore. The agents radioed Sheriff Jess and asked him to send out the game warden via water patrol. They were certain they were not going to be able to apprehend the driver of the vessel. The agents hopped out of their Chevy Avalanche and started walking towards the Jeep.

"Hey fellas, beautiful day isn't it!"

The driver of the Jeep turned towards them looking at them suspiciously.

"Sure is guys! What can I do for ya?"

About that time, the boat owner hopped back into his

vessel and took off westwardly towards the US 59 bridge that crosses the Trinity River. The driver of the Jeep started to reach into his truck when the agent pulled his Glock and pointed it at him.

"I wouldn't do that if I were you. Put your hands up, you are under arrest for trafficking moonshine here in San Jacinto County."

The man jumped into his Jeep and the agents ran behind the Chevy Avalanche taking cover. The Jeep revved up and started to head towards the road, leading back to the main gate, when one of the agents pointed his weapon at the front driver's side tire of the vehicle and shot off three rounds. The Jeep rolled a couple of times in the sand and threw the driver out. The agents ran over to the driver, checked for injuries determining he was only a bit dazed. They cuffed him and read him his rights.

Sirens were blazing down the river. The game warden was chasing the flat bottom that had been on the sandbar only minutes earlier. The flat bottom landed on the sandbar and the driver jumped out and started running in the direction of the agents. One of them pointed his Glock at the boat captain.

"Lay face down with your hands over your head!"

The game warden walked over, handcuffed the guy and waited for backup to take him down to the station.

After a few hours of questioning, the agents determined the Jeep driver was a local hoodlum by the name of Harry "Mud

Bug" Young. He was one of those local guys who didn't do anything honest for a living. He was constantly looking for the next quick fix and would sell anything illegal as long as it was worth a significant amount of money. Evidently, he and the flat bottom captain Robert "Bert" Robertson were running moonshine up the river supplying hooch to the Drew's Landing Campground across the Trinity River in Goodrich. It was a lucrative deal as the campground owner would pay Bert for the delivery and then sell it for a premium to the campers staying there.

Ambush

Ouida was looking forward to a good day of business and ultimate peace and quiet for whatever that meant in Ouida's world. It was six-thirty in the morning and the sun had not yet peeked over the piney wood treetops when Ouida stepped into her icehouse to prepare for the day. She took the trash out from the night before and tossed it into the dumpster next to the bar. She counted the proceeds from that same evening and put the receivables into a white bank bag etched with the name "First State Bank" across it. She walked out back of the bar, over to her F-150 and placed the bank bag under the seat planning to make a deposit later in the day. She stepped back into the rear door of the icehouse when a voice from the corner of the bar called to her.

"Shut that door bitch or I'll blow your mother fuckin' head off."

Ouida shut the door and looked in the direction of where the voice came from.

"Who the goddamn hell are you?"

"Oh you know me lover girl. Now take your ass into the main room and stand over by that pool table right now."

Ouida walked over to the pool table nervously, unsure of

what was happening or who the voice belonged to. She kept thinking she had heard it before yet could not put her finger on it.

"Turn your fuckin' ass around and face the pool table bitch!"

"I don't know who you are but I put the money in my truck under the seat. You can go the fuck out there and get what you need. I don't want any goddamn trouble around here."

"Oh, money ain't what I want you stupid motherfucker. I'm here to give you what's comin' to you because of the fuck ass way you treated me with disrespect the last time we met."

Then it dawned on Ouida.

"Fuckin' Coco."

Coco walked up to Ouida and the click of a switchblade echoed out across the bar. She grabbed Ouida's hair and pulled her face up to her own. She then stuck the tip of the knife to Ouida's cheek.

"I'm goin' to mark your fuckin' ass up so everyone in this county knows that you are mine and no one else's. You feel me bitch?"

Ouida's .38 special was out of reach behind the bar. A sense of fear rose up in her.

"Now, Coco. You know I didn't mean any harm back there. I was under a lot of pressure being arrested and all for somethin' I did not do. With you addin' to the pressure wantin' to be my girlfriend and all, I just lost it. I was totally out of my right mind that day and you really should consider givin' me a goddamn break."

With that, Ouida broke free of Coco's grip and ran to the other side of the pool table and grabbed a stick.

"Now, I'm pretty damn good with these shooters and I'll take your mother fuckin' rug munchin' wetback ass out if you don't put that damn blade down now bitch!"

Coco hopped up on the pool table and lunged at Ouida. Ouida swung the heavy side of the pool cue at Coco's legs catching her off balance. Coco fell off the pool table and hit the concrete floor with a crack. She let out a large yelp.

"Bitch, you better be runnin' cuz I'm gunna cut you real good now!"

Coco hopped up onto her feet and chased Ouida across the bar. She picked up one of the chairs and threw it at Ouida popping Ouida on her back laying her face flat on the floor. As she lay there all she could think about was getting off that nasty bar floor that was covered in years of sticky stale beer and cigarette ashes. She started to crawl to the end of the bar when Coco caught her legs and whipped her over on her backside. Ouida was once again face-to-face with Coco in a very compromising position. Coco hovered over Ouida and put the blade right up against her cheek. She pinned Ouida down and cut a letter "C" into her left cheek with the razor sharp blade.

Ouida screamed in pain as the blood trickled down the side of her face.

"Now, bitch, that's from me and all the world will know that you are fuckin' mine!"

Adrenaline kicked in and Ouida kicked Coco off her. She jumped on top of Coco and pinned her to the ground. She grabbed both sides of her head with her fingers entwined in Coco's cornrows.

"You really want a piece of me don't you, you fuckin' bitch? Well, here's a piece of me you won't forget for a long time cuz you just don't damn well know who the mother fuckin' hell you are dealin' with and on account I am PMS-in'. I'm goin' to make sure you get a little extra dose of me so you don't forget this encounter today you sorry ass mutherfucker!"

Ouida balled her fist up and knocked Coco square between the eyes. Coco threw her legs up and locked them around Ouida's neck wrestling style. She laid Ouida flat on her back once again knocking over a few barstools in the process. Hopping on top of Ouida, she continued knocking the shit out of her as if she were a punching bag. With each hit, the room became dimmer and dimmer for Ouida. She was doing everything she could to get Coco off of her to no avail. Suddenly, the lights went out.

A short while later, Ouida awakened. She was laying on the bar floor covered in stink and blood. She could barely see out of her right eye and tasted a considerable amount of blood gushing out of her mouth. Coco was looking down at her.

"Paybacks are hell, bitch. I wanted to wait around long enough to remind you of why it is I paid you this friendly mother fuckin' visit this fine fuckin' mornin'. You need to know that I am aware of your every damn move. I am watchin' you every second of every minute of every hour of every goddamn day. I will show up in a moments notice and mess your pretty face up worse than I did today. So I want you to understand this isn't the last time you will see me and between now and then, you ain't gonna find me either. If you go off and tell the police who did this to you, I will come find you sooner than you think. You understand me you fuckin' piece of no good shit?"

"Whack!" Coco's body froze. Her eyes rolled back in her head and she slumped on top of Ouida. Ouida laid there a moment scared out of her ever loving mind. A boot kicked Coco off of Ouida and a hand stretched over to help her up. Ouida grabbed the hand and as she was lifted off the floor as voice spoke up.

"Precious one, you look like you have had a very tough morning. Dear Jesus! We need to get you to a doctor pronto. There's some things that need to be tended to on that purty face of yours."

Dwanna gave Coco a couple of hard kicks in her side just to make sure she wasn't getting up anytime soon. Dwanna went around the bar, grabbed a plastic bag and filled it with ice. She also grabbed a clean towel, dampened it from the sink and returned to Ouida who was now sitting on a barstool staring off in a daze.

"Now Ouida Mae, I need you to look at me and let me know how you are feeling!"

Dwanna began wiping the blood from Ouida's face.

"Now, take this icepack and place it over that eye so we can get some of the swelling down."

Dwanna picked up the telephone.

"Hello, Sheriff Jess please."

"Sheriff Jess here."

"Hi Sheriff, this here's Dwanna Crabb and I'm at Ouida Lawless' icehouse. Seems she has run into a bit of trouble this morning and it appears we are going to need someone to pick up this piece of trash lying on Ouida's floor over here and possibly an ambulance on account Ouida needs some medical attention."

Ouida looked at Dwanna.

"Please no ambulance, caint you just take me to the hospital?"

"Scratch the ambulance, I'll take care of the transport but we do need someone down here to take care of this bitch on the floor."

Ouida looked over at Dwanna surprised to hear any curse word come out of her saintly mouth. Dwanna looked at Ouida understanding what she was thinking.

"We all have our moments! Praise be to God!"

Ten minutes later Sheriff Jess and another deputy stepped into the icehouse. He walked over to Ouida.

"What in the hell happened to you girl?"

Dwanna motioned to Ouida not to talk since her face was so damn messed up and any movement might cause more pain.

"Apparently, this here Coco met Ouida when she was in jail a while back for that moonshine stuff. Coco took it upon herself to try to convince Ouida this morning that she was going to make her life miserable. As you can see, Sheriff Jess, she did her best. I was driving by the icehouse and noticed the "Open" sign wasn't on yet which was not typical of Ouida. So, I decided to come on in and make sure she was all right. I just had a feeling in my spirit that things weren't ok. That's when I happened quietly upon this woman here beating the you know what out of Ouida. I grabbed a pool cue and whopped her over the head with it and she hit the ground in nothing flat. I'm surprised I still have it in me to deliver a wollup like that. Anyhow, she's been out cold for about twenty minutes and probably needs a bit of medical attention herself."

Sheriff Jess asked the deputy to try to rouse Coco. He then walked over to Ouida and assessed her physical condition.

"Girl, she sure did make a mess of you this morning. I'm no doctor but I don't think there will be any permanent damage other than a battle scar from that cut on your cheek. Why don't you and Dwanna head on off to the hospital and I'll put a sign on your door here that you are closed today and will re-open tomorrow?"

Ouida nodded her head ok and started crying. Dwanna put her arm around Ouida and led her out to the car. Ouida laid out on the backseat and held the icepack to her face while Dwanna drove her to the Memorial Medical Center Emergency Room in Livingston.

The doctor emerged from the exam room and called out to Dwanna. Dwanna ran over to him.

"It's not as serious as it looks. Her eye is going to be fine once the swelling goes down. We will assess whether there is any injury to her vision in a few days. She does have a slight concussion and will need to be monitored over the next 24 hours. Does she have anyone who can stay with her during that time?"

"Yes, doctor, I'll be able to take care of her. Thank you so much for tending to her this morning."

Dwanna turned to Ouida and put her arm around her leading her out to the car.

"Good Lord, that Coco really has it out for you girl. I know this isn't very consoling right now, but you really need to be more careful Ouida! I thought I was gunna scream when I caught her standing over you ready to give you another blow to that pretty ole face of yours!"

Ouida looked at Dwanna all puffy eyed black and blue.

"I don't know how I will ever thank you enough for what you did for me this mornin'. I surely thought I was good as dead! I just couldn't get the upper hand on that goddamn bitch for the life of me! I just hope Sheriff Jess is gunna find a way to put her in the big house for a while over this."

Dwanna drove Ouida on to her house so she could keep an eye on her overnight ensuring she wasn't suffering too terribly from the concussion.

The phone rang at Dwanna's later that evening.

"Hello, this is Dwanna."

"Hello Dwanna, this is Sheriff Jess."

"It's so good to hear from you this evening Sheriff Jess."

"Well, Dwanna, I just wanted to check in and see how things went with Ouida this afternoon at the emergency room."

"Ouida has a concussion and is staying here tonight so I can keep an eye on her."

"Well, how is she mentally, Dwanna?"

"She's fair to midland Sheriff. She has a terrible headache and is pretty banged up. However, the swelling and brusing should go down in the next few days. I think her ego is a bit battered."

"OK, I'm glad she is with you."

"What did y'all do with that Coco woman?"

"Well, we booked her for attempted murder and had her face the judge quickly thereafter before we locked her up for the night. She pled self-defense of course so we will need to get a deposition from Ouida as soon as we can so that she doesn't forget what all happened this morning. I also expect this will need to go to trial. I'm glad we took pictures of Ouida before you both headed to the emergency room. We also took pictures of the icehouse and the wreck that Coco made of it."

"Well, I hope the judge understands she was there to kill Ouida and had every intent to do so if I hadn't stepped in."

"Dwanna, we will also need a deposition from you as to the moment you drove by the icehouse until the moment you brought her home from the emergency room."

"Oh no, am I going to get into trouble for knocking Coco out?"

"No ma'am, You were absolutely acting in defense of Ouida and will not be charged with anything. We just need you as a witness."

"Well, I will sit down tonight and write everything I can about what happened when I arrived. I'll also try to get Ouida to recount what happened and get it on paper also. I just hope the Lord Jesus is sending his messenger angel to that Coco woman letting her know that what she has done is not right and that He is not pleased with her actions."

Dwanna hung up the phone and checked in on Ouida

finding her snoring loud as an old coon dog. She picked up the phone and called her prayer chain asking them to keep Ouida and that woman Coco in their prayers.

"Please ask the Lord that Ouida would heal quickly and the memory of this would not impair her life one bit and that by this experience she would come to know our Sweet Jesus even more. For Coco, pray that she would see the error of her ways, repent and seek the Lord's forgiveness. Also that she would spend a long time in prison for what she has done so that no one else would get hurt."

Texas Tea Audit

The next morning Tater's daddy showed up and wanted to have a private meeting with her. She had him come into the office and shut the door behind them.

"Tater darlin', I've been reviewing your books and things just aren't adding up. You know I keep wondering why you are running an extra truck but there is no record of sales off that vehicle and you don't have enough inventory to be sending out an extra truck right yet."

"Let me see what you have there Daddy. I'm glad we put those RFID chips on them to track their whereabouts. However, I thought we were accounting for them all. Tell you what I will do, I'll have Marvin pull the logs to determine when the extra truck is leaving the lot and where it is going specifically. I'll also do some poking around the yard and see if I can't figure out what's going on. There's got to be a simple explanation to this."

"Ok honey, I suspect it's probably something very logical but just want to make sure the books align as we have our board meeting with the investors next month and I want to show them how well you are doing here. Here's a copy of what I have. Let me know what you find out in the next couple of days if you would sweetheart."

"I certainly will Daddy. Thanks so much for coming by and bringing this to my attention!"

Tater walked her daddy out and met up with Cueball and Patty in the yard. They were running around like chickens with their heads cut off as this was the busiest day of the week. Cueball stopped by Tater to catch his breath.

"How's Mr. Murphy today?"

"He's fine Cue, told me to tell you and Patty hello. He had to head on out for a meeting."

Tater walked out to the yard and counted up her rigs. Five in total. Four to make the runs each week and one on standby in the event an extra run was needed. She walked over to the rig and on the bottom right corner of the driver's door was the number 5 etched on it. She didn't have to climb in but noticed that it appeared to be a bit dirtier than expected since all it really did was sit in the yard day to day.

Patty came around the corner.

"Hey, Ms. Tater. Want to hop in?"

"No thanks Patty. Have we had a need to send all our trucks on deliveries within the last month? I'm taking inventory and want to confirm whether or not we have had all trucks operating?"

"Well, this truck has gone out once a week to that new account over there in Coldspring. We figured it would be best to send this one on that short haul since it wasn't being used anyway. Hate to see equipment just sit and rot like it could have."

"That is good to know Patty. Thank you for the heads up. I think that was a wise move on you and Cue's part."

Tater walked back to her office and picked up the phone.

"Marvin, we need to talk. Can you come out here on Friday as usual and spend a little extra time with me going over the logs? We have an investors meeting next month and I need to make sure our data is aligning with the log books and account sales. Also, can you provide me with the routes tied to each truck's RFID chips? I will need to balance that out with the sales and accounts because you know my Daddy will want that information."

"Absolutely Tater. I'll be there around 10am on Friday."

"Great, see you then Marvin."

Tater looked up her client list and found Lake Livingston Dam Marina listed on her weekly routes. Tater recalled adding this business to her client list as they were receiving oil to use for their boat repair business they had going on there. Patty was friends with the owner and persuaded Tater to sell them product for their repair business as well as to sell their own branded oil out of their storefront. Tater thought it was a good idea to get some of the locals involved in her business and to generate interest with some of the marinas up and down Lake Livingston, Lake Conroe and Lake Houston. She was fairly certain this aligned with Patty's explanation and was simply going to check this with the data Marvin provided her on Friday.

Agent Horton gave Sheriff Jess a visit to catch him up on the events around the moonshine operation investigation. Sheriff Jess met him in the lobby of the police station and motioned him to come into his office.

"Take a seat Agent Horton. So glad to hear you all are making progress on the investigation."

"The woman we arrested over on Robin Lane last week is Mrs. Belinda Banks."

"Yes, I know of Mrs. Banks. She's an interesting character."

"She apparently wasn't a medical transcriptionist after all and used her residence to store cases of moonshine and distribute to the local sales branch."

"'Sales branch' huh Agent?"

"An additional delivery driver and the manager out at the recycling operation on US 59 was also arrested. We have also made quite a bit of headway in questioning the folks we brought in and had some very solid tips on the details surrounding the operation."

"You all certainly have been busy. Is there anything I can do to help?"

"The main thing outstanding is to actually catch the person

or persons manufacturing the stuff. We just haven't arrived at that conclusion yet Sheriff, but we are certain it's going on right under your nose."

"What's the plan for those who have been arrested Agent Horton?"

"We are keeping them in custody until the investigation is complete. They will probably plea a deal in the event everything goes the way they have described it."

"Well, that's a shame Agent Horton."

"You know how it works Sheriff. Mrs. Banks, however, isn't talking so she won't be going anywhere real soon. We will need to stake out the area for the next few days and will keep in touch with you. If you don't mind, I would like to have an agent here at the station to take incoming intel during that time as well."

"My office and personnel are at your disposal Agent Horton."

"Thank you Sheriff, we appreciate your cooperation and assistance."

"Breaker, breaker 1-9. Papa Bear you twenty?"

"10-4 Captn' Clyde."

"Looks like we got bear in the bush, so stay on the lookout."

"Bear in the bush, huh? This should be a fun day of

hunting then."

"Well, howdy Veggie Man."

"Howdy Papa Bear. Howdy Clyde."

"Gotta love a great hunt when it involves bear around here."

"That's right, Papa Bear. Wanted you all to be aware there is something brewing here in town. Over and Out."

"Over and Out Captn' Clyde, Veggie Man."

Mr. Lobo walked into the kitchen and explained to Mrs. Carol there would probably be some excitement around the county for the next couple of days. She looked at him and threw him one of her mischievous smiles.

"Ya don't say!"

Tater had been pouring over her records for a couple of days after she gave Marvin a call. She realized today was the day her Coldspring tanker was going out on delivery. She stepped outside and found Patty talking to the driver and waving him out the lot.

"Later, Kody."

Kody winked and waved as he headed down FM 1127. Patty turned to find Tater standing next to her.

"That's our Coldspring delivery I was tellin' you about the other day Tater. One full load each week carried off to the marina. I hear they got a really amazin' setup out there with all the lake traffic they get in over the weekend and the repair shop they have operatin'. The American Legion, across the street from the marina, is havin' a bike rally that starts tonight and runs through the entire weekend. Bikers are coming in from all over Texas, Oklahoma and Louisiana."

"Well, isn't that something? You and Cherokee headed up there anytime this weekend?"

"We are definitely goin' to be up there for the fundraiser they're havin' for one of the guys who got hurt in a bike accident last month. He's a good friend of Cherokee's."

"Sounds like it's goin' to be a big to-do over there then. Well, gotta get back to the paperwork Patty, see ya later."

Tater headed back into the office and caught the phone as it was ringing.

"Tater, I've got the info you need for the books and will be headed out there in about an hour."

"Beep, Beep," signaled the brown UPS truck. The gate leading into Mrs. Banks yard was open so the driver pulled on through. He exited the truck and stepped onto her porch when Agent Weems swung it wide open and met him with a big shit eating grin on her face.

"Hit the ground with your hands behind your head. You are under arrest for the trafficking of moonshine."

She handcuffed he guy and read him his Miranda rights and

introduced herself and Agent Thompson.

"Now, we are going to sit you down right here and you are going to tell us everything you know. Otherwise, you will regret the day you were born. However, you will get a fine opportunity to make friends with the folks down in the Houston lockup."

She and Agent Thompson promptly led the driver into the kitchen and shut the door behind them. The agents had set up a sting operation at Old Lady Bank's house to apprehend more delivery drivers and gain more clarity on the operation. "Beep, Beep," signaled the second truck. The driver pulled into the yard, exited the vehicle and was greeted by Agent Walters.

"Hands up, you are under arrest."

The driver turned to run. He stopped when he heard Agent Walters pull the slide back on his semi-automatic.

"I would advise you not to take another step."

Agent Walters walked up behind the man and gave him a gentle nudge into the house. Agent Walters then explained why he was under arrest as he handcuffed him and subsequently read him his Miranda rights. He and Agent Horton led the suspect into the bedroom and shut the door behind them. About an hour later, Agent Horton and Agent Weems re-emerged and compared stories which were identical to one another.

Agent Horton was dressed in a brown uniform similar to the drivers. He and Agent Weems went outside to take stock of the inventory in the trucks. The inventory in the first truck was loaded into the second vehicle. An unmarked car turned the corner with two officers inside. One got out and stepped into the driver's side of the second delivery truck. He started up the engine and headed to Houston in the vehicle loaded with evidence. Agent Horton hopped into the first delivery truck, Agent Weems stepped in the back along with the driver of the unmarked car and drove down Robin Lane, turned south onto Jesse Lane then steered right onto FM 1127 towards US 59. Meanwhile, Agent Thompson and Agent Walters packed up the suspects and loaded them into another unmarked car and headed into Houston.

Agent Horton took a right on US 59 and headed north towards Goodrich via the 393 cutoff. He passed the Family Life Church and hung a left on FM 1988. A few miles down the road he veered left onto 3278 and pulled up by the fuel pumps at the Lake Livingston Dam Marina. Mr. Embry's boy Tank stepped out.

"Come on round back, we've got quite a load for you today."

Agent Horton pulled around and backed up to the loading dock. He hopped out of the truck and approached Tank.

"I'm here on official business and it would behoove you to step into the back of this truck and mind your P's and Q's."

One of the doors to the delivery truck swung open, he pushed Tank into the truck and Agent Weems promptly handcuffed him while reading him his Miranda rights. She left him there with the undercover agent. She quietly got out of the truck and walked over to the marina store. By then, Agent Horton had slipped into the men's bathroom and changed into his standard jeans, t-shirt and boots paraphernalia. He looked over at Agent Weems.

"Hey hot momma, what you got for me today?"

"Hey, Sugah. I haven't seen you around these here parts in a while."

Mr. Embry looked up from behind the counter and started laughing at the antics of the two.

"Where you kids from?"

"Oh, we're from Crockett. We came down here for the bike rally and fundraiser."

"I heard they are catchin' a mess of crappie up off the east fork today. Can I interest you two lovebirds in some adult beverages and bait?"

A patrol car pulled up to the marina and Sheriff Jess stepped out. He entered the front door and looked over at Mr. Embry.

"Bud, how you doin' today?"

"Doin' good Jess. Yourself?"

"OK, considering. I need you to come over here and talk to me for a minute. I'm sure these two won't mind waiting."

Sheriff Jess took Mr. Embry to the marina office and shut

the door behind them. "Bud, you know why I'm here today?"

"Well, Jess, I reckon you came to get a cup of that good coffee I serve here."

"I wish that were true Bud."

"What is it Jess?"

"Well, we have had an investigation going on here in the county for quite a while now and apparently it has led us to you."

Mr. Embry began fidgeting and rubbing his brow. Sweat glistened from his forehead and his face and neck burned red.

"Now Bud, this is what's going to happen today. We want to ensure this investigation goes on without a hitch, you understand me?"

Mr. Embry nodded his head yes.

"It would be in your best interest Bud to act your usual self. Don't think about doing anything rash around here or I will shut you down faster than you can call your momma."

Mr. Embry's eyes widened then he nodded his head in agreement indicating he would follow Sheriff Jess' directive. Mr. Embry and Sheriff Jess emerged from the office and Mr. Embry stepped behind the counter. He looked up at Agent Weems and Agent Horton. They brought over a bait bucket, cast net, a couple of homemade breakfast tacos and two cups of coffee handing Mr. Embry a credit card as payment. Mr. Embry rung them up and they promptly headed over to one of the porch picnic tables to polish off the tacos and coffee as they waited on the delivery.

Knock, knock went a rap on the office door back at Texas Tea, LLC.

"Come in."

Marvin walked in with his laptop and a fresh batch of kolaches from Shipley donuts. The smell of fresh yeast dough wrapped around steaming hot jalapeño sausage was the worst temptation of the morning.

"You came bearing gifts did you?"

Marvin grinned and nodded his head yes.

"Well, I hope you brought me one of those ham and cheese ones. Let's get down to business."

Marvin popped open his Macbook Pro and attached it to the monitor on Tater's desk. He pulled up the RFID tracking detail and pointed out the routes aligned with her client list. Marvin scratched his head.

"What Marvin?"

"Well, it just seems odd to me that the number five truck is making runs at all. All this truck does is take a trip each Friday over to the Lake Livingston Dam Marina. What would the Marina want with your product?"

"Well, you know they have that repair shop they run over there and most of the repair work in this county comes to them with their big operation. Evidently they are taking a delivery each week and using three-fourths of it for repairs and selling the other fourth in their own branded containers to make a little extra money through their general store."

"Tell me what are you getting paid for each shipment Tater?"

"They are paying the tier two rate since they are a sole proprietorship and are right here in our back yard."

"I found the glitch here. Unit five was never added properly to the logs. Give me a few minutes and I will add this route."

"Well, that's a relief. Daddy was questioning some gaps in the books and I think this pretty much solves this dilemma as we can account for the activity of the tanker, justify the route and prove payment on the product. Marvin, you've been a great help to me today and I truly appreciate it."

It was eight in the morning and the sunrise was bouncing off the top of Lake Livingston outside the Damn Marina. The sky couldn't be any clearer and the air any fresher that mild morning. The Texas Tea, LLC tanker pulled in and the driver got out and connected the loading hose to the underground storage unit. When he was done fueling the tank, he stepped into the marina store and walked over to Mr. Embry. Mr. Embry looked up.

"Hey Kody, how you doin' today?"

"Doin' good Mr. Embry. Here's your invoice."

Mr. Embry signed the bottom of the invoice and gave Kody back his copy handing him an envelope.

"Here's a little extra for the hard work."

Sheriff Jess held the front door open and let Kody through tipping his hat and wishing him a good day. As Kody was stepping up to the cab of the truck, Agent Weems came around the corner.

"Hands up! You are under arrest for the trafficking of moonshine."

Kody threw his hands up and Agent Weems promptly cuffed him, read him his Miranda rights and put him in the back of Sheriff Jess' patrol car. Sheriff Jess looked at Mr. Embry.

"Bud, I think it's time to lock up for the day don't you?"

Mr. Embry nodded his head and followed Sheriff Jess out the front door.

"Now, let's go on over to the service warehouse and see what kind of operation you have going on."

Mr. Embry, Sheriff Jess and Agent Horton promptly walked into the three thousand square foot warehouse. Inside they found a pump that led from the outside underground storage tank into the workshop. It was connected by a clever arrangement of hoses that were used to fill multiple mason jars at a time. Next to the unit were assembled cardboard boxes containing quart size mason jars filled to the rim ready for shipment. Sheriff Jess radioed the station and told them to dispatch a couple of vans out to Lake Livingston Dam Marina to inventory and confiscate the equipment. Sheriff Jess looked at Mr. Embry.

"Bud, you and I go way back. I would never have imagined you would have somethin' like this goin' on around here. I think you and Agent Horton are goin' to become really good friends over the next few hours. Agent Horton, he's all yours."

Agent Horton cuffed Mr. Embry, read him his Miranda rights and stuffed him into the unmarked car which also contained his son Tank. Tank Embry, Mr. Embry and Kody were shipped back to Houston for further questioning. Sheriff Jess picked up his phone.

"Tater Baby, I'm headed over to see you. You available now?"

BUSTED

Tater hung up the phone and looked over at Marvin.

"Who was that Tater?"

"That was Uncle Jess. He evidently has something he needs to speak with me about."

Cueball stuck his head in the door and yelled.

"Shit! Tater! Get out here please!"

Tater and Marvin went running out the front of the office onto the porch where Patty was standing there holding Coon-Ass Joe's dog Gomer laying limp in their arms.

"I think he's been paisened Tater!"

"Poisoned?"

Marvin walked over to the two, picked Gomer up and threw back his head and let out a whistle as a result of the smell of Gomer's breath.

"He's not poisoned, or at least I don't think he is. He smells three sheets to the wind. Seems he has been hitting the hooch overtime again."

Tater and the gang heard sirens heading down FM 1127. They all jumped to the side of the parking lot as the patrol cars turned into the drive of Texas Tea, LLC. Tater and crew did a double-take only to find Sheriff Jess and several deputies step out of their vehicles. Sheriff Jess approached them.

"Tater Murphy, you and your crew are under arrest!"

"Arrest? For what Uncle Jess?"

"You all are under arrest for trafficking moonshine."

Tater looked up at Sheriff Jess bewildered. She then looked over at her crew and scratched her head.

The agents stepped forward and handcuffed, Tater, Marvin, Patty and Cueball reading them their Miranda rights. Everyone was escorted into the office and put in separate rooms for questioning. Sheriff Jess and Agent Thompson led Tater into her office and shut the door behind them.

"Tater, we were on a sting operation over at the Dam this morning and one of your tankers pulled up chocked full of moonshine."

"How in the hell did one of my trucks end up with a delivery of moonshine? Where in the heck did they get that stuff? I do not manufacture nor distribute moonshine Uncle Jess!"

"Darlin', that's what we are goin' to find out right now. We really have to suspect everyone here but expect complete cooperation knowin' that you are not the one to blame in this matter. So just go along with us and let's see what we can find out. I'm goin' to have to keep you handcuffed for the time bein'."

Gomer had followed them into Tater's office. He jumped

up against Sheriff Jess attracted to the dog treat Jess had left in his pocket. Sheriff retrieved the bone and stuck it in Gomer's mouth. About that time he got a big whiff of Gomer's breath and looked up at Tater.

"Looks like Gomer has been nipping on the moonshine Tater."

"Well, funny that you mention it. He's been hanging around here a lot lately Uncle Jess."

"I think it's time we take a walk around the property Tater. Let's see if Gomer can't lead the way."

Sheriff Jess, Agent Thompson and Tater went outside and started walking the property. Agent Thompson reached down and picked up a handful of corn kernels.

"Tater, do you find it interesting that you have corn all over this side of your drive?"

"Well, we had talked about it but explained it away as the corn delivery busted a bag en route to the pig rancher down the road. In retrospect, we have seen this happen on various occasions lately as well."

Sheriff Jess looked over at Gomer. The old dog was steadying himself on his wobbly legs while making his way over to the third processing unit Tater had recently added to grow the business. Gomer instantly began licking the outtake valve. Sheriff Jess walked over to the unit, ran his fingers around the outtake valve then put them up to his nose taking a sniff.

"Whooooo Tater Murphy! This is as damn pure as it gets around these parts."

He walked back over to Tater and gave her a whiff and she just about passed out not from the fumes but from shock that this could happen on her watch. Tater then asked Sheriff Jess if he would mind bringing Marvin into her office. She had some things she would like to show him and Agent Thompson as far as the books were concerned. They all returned to her office and a few minutes later Marvin came walking in with Agent Thompson. Tater looked at him.

"Hey Marvin, you wouldn't be able to bring up those logs from the processors now would you?"

"Well, let me… "

Agent Thompson sat down at the desk, grabbed the MacBook Pro from Marvin and popped the lid open.

"I've got quite a bit of experience dealing with technical forensic matters. Let me see what I can find out here."

Sheriff Jess put Marvin in a chair on the opposite side of the room and sat right next to him. After a couple of hours Agent Thompson looked up.

"This is where you weren't able to see the difference Tater. Your log books did show your standard routes, the four tankers and the output of your two processors. The RFID chips revealed the discovery of the fifth tanker transporting materials. The logical explanation was the tanker was being used to handle the small delivery each week. However, you overlooked one minute detail, the output did not line up with the deliveries. That's where your books were actually off. That tanker was leaving out of here with a delivery from processor three and it wasn't hitting your books."

Suddenly, Tater looked over at Marvin who was staring at the floor shaking his head. Sheriff Jess looked at Marvin.

"That is exactly what Marvin and I were discussing this morning Agent Thompson. However, he negated the fact the tanker was filling up from processor 3."

Sheriff Jess patted Marvin on his arm.

"Well, son, I think you have some explaining to do here."

Agent Thompson removed the handcuffs from Tater and sent her into the waiting area. Tater looked at her Uncle Jess with tears in her eyes and walked out of the office.

Agent Thompson leaned over to Marvin.

"So tell me Marvin, what is it about you techie types that can sure turn on a dime and run the wrong way? Did you know that we ran a background check on all of Tater's crew here and found you were the one who stuck out like a sore thumb? You've been dabbling in other stuff for quite a while and thought you would hit the big times with this, didn't you?"

Sheriff Jess chimed in.

"Who was it here that helped you with this operation? Who was it here that had connections to others in this operation?

Well, these are rhetorical questions of course because we ran the plates of all the delivery trucks and vehicles involved in this moonshine trafficking scheme and we found one common thread. The owner of the vehicles was also the driver of the Friday delivery to the Lake Livingston Marina. So let's take a look at these here surveillance tapes and see what we can't dig up. Oh and don't you worry, those tapes you deleted, Agent Thompson knows how to retrieve them since they were stored in the cloud. And although you didn't have time to delete the one from this morning, we can take a look at that one first."

Agent Thompson took a couple of hours pouring over the surveillance video and looked up at Sheriff Jess.

"Sheriff, take a look at this interesting tidbit of information."

He carried the laptop over to Sheriff Jess and showed him the images of Patty stepping up to the driver's side window of the cab of unit 5. Kody handed her a thick envelope and she gave him a big kiss right as Tater was stepping out of the front door onto the porch. Sheriff Jess looked in amazement and could see how the pieces of the puzzle were coming together.

"So darn disappointing. Patty had a squeaky clean record until today."

Patty and Cueball were led into the office along with Tater. Cueball looked over at Tater. Patty kept her sights set on the floor. Tater's eyes were almost swollen shut from crying.

Cueball started crying just at the sight of Tater crying. Agent Thompson walked over to Cueball and sat him down.

"Do you have any idea what has gone on around here Cue?"

"Well, the agent was questioning me about any suspicious activity on the lot over the past few months and I told him that I didn't know of anything. That we had everything set up tight around here where no one could steal any of our equipment or nothin' like that. I also told him how I had trained Patty up to come in durin' the early hours of the mornin' and set the yard up and I took the late shift makin' sure everything was shut down tight before headin' out each evenin'."

"So, you must have trained her very well and had a lot of trust in her to provide her with keys to the property?"

"Yes sir. She is very trustworthy."

Patty looked up at the Agent and her face turned redder than the hair on Tater's head. Agent Thompson walked over to Cueball and removed the handcuffs from his wrists. He sent Cueball and Tater back out into the lobby to wait a bit longer.

Cueball put on a new pot of coffee and grabbed one of the last kolaches out of the box on the counter. He sat on the couch next to Tater and offered her a bite. She shook her head no and started crying again. Cueball put the food down and grabbed a box of Kleenex and handed her one.

"Tater, you gotta know that I had no idea this was going

on!"

"I know Cue, I know."

Tater burst out in tears. Cueball grabbed her and gave her a big hug holding her until she quieted down.

"It's gunna be all right Tater. Don't you worry. It looks like this entire thing had nothin' to do with you directly and so your name will still be good in these parts."

"Daddy is going to be so furious with me Cue. He had trusted me with this business and I missed the most important detail of all. He came over here the other day saying the books didn't line up. I had Marvin come visit me today to help me figure them out. Then, just when I thought everything was settled. . .BAM! We all get cuffed and accused of trafficking moonshine for goodness sakes!"

Tater let out another cry and buried her face in her hands continuing to sob away. Meanwhile, Sheriff Jess and Agent Thompson were questioning Patty further. She and Marvin were sitting side by side at that point.

"Sheriff, you know how times is so hard. I needed to make extry money fer my granbabies who don't have nuthin' to eat. Not to mention I don't have no insurance to pay for my diverticulitis treatments. You know how expensive medical treatment can be Sheriff."

Sheriff Jess and Agent Thompson looked at each other and shook their heads.

"Patty, you do know we read you your rights and you have the right to an attorney?"

"I don't need an attorney Mr. FBI Agent whatever your name is."

Agent Weems entered the office, walked over to Marvin and escorted him into a separate room for questioning.

Sheriff Jess leaned over to Patty.

"Can you tell me how you know Kody?"

"Well, me and Kody Nash were childhood sweethearts. I was able to get him a job drivin' fer Tater. He and I were havin' a beer at Ouida's icehouse one day after work and we got the bright idea of how that empty processor was goin' to waste just sittin' there. Then, it dawned on me, we could make moonshine out of that thing and make a pretty penny to boot."

"Is that right Patty? And how in the world would you know how to make moonshine?"

"Well, can't be any more difficult than when I worked at the brewery down in Houston for two years. Need the right ingredients, flip the switch and the processor does the rest of the work."

Agent Thompson turned to Marvin.

"Ok Marvin, let's talk about how you got involved in this operation. Remember, you too have been read your rights and can call your attorney."

"I have nothing to hide. I was not the mastermind behind

this operation. Kody and Patty blackmailed me into messing with the records by hiding the moonshine business from Tater and her daddy. I was at the office one early morning working on the new processing unit's motherboard when Kody approached me. Kody found out that I was working for a competing company and using the same technology and tracking system that Tater was using. I had not divulged to her that her information was being stored on the same database which, in turn, made me extra money on my contract. Kody knew this was a conflict of interest and if I didn't want to lose my job with Tater then I better work with Kody and Patty on this new venture."

In the meantime, two other agents were dispatched to Marvin's office in The Woodlands, Texas to confiscate his equipment and formally investigate the allegations against him. They found that Marvin had quite the setup in his tiny office off Research Forest Drive. He didn't have any mainframe systems in place as he was using cloud computing to store his data. They were able to confirm that he had ownership of the data for Texas Tea, LLC yet also had a corresponding account with the code name "White Lightning" which the agents were able to electronically track back to processor three on Tater's property.

Agent Thompson and Weems drove Marvin and Patty to the lockup in Houston.

Mr. Murphy stepped into Tater's office. He found Cueball

and Sheriff Jess consoling Tater. She looked up at her daddy with swollen eyes, a raw red nose and a defeated spirit. Cueball looked over at Murphy.

"I've done everythang I can to try to console her but I just can't get her to stop cryin!"

"Tater Baby, it's going to be all right. You are in the clear and thank God Cueball is too. We just need to shut things down for a couple of weeks for them to complete their investigation. Just think of this time as a sort of vacation."

Tater looked up at Mr. Murphy.

"Daddy, I just really feel like I have failed you! How in the world did I miss this stuff going on right under my nose?"

Tater began squalling again. Her daddy swooped her into his arms giving her time to cry it all out.

Moonshine Gossip

The smell of cherry pie and the sweetness of Sallie Jean was the only thing Cueball had on his mind that dreary winter afternoon. As Cueball stepped into the diner, Sallie Jean met him with that warm, glowing smile only she could provide.

"Hello honey. You look like you have had a heck of a day Cue."

"Oh Sallie Jean, it's been horrible! I was almost thrown in jail for the craziest scheme that has ever happened down here in Shepherd."

Sallie Jean sat down next to Cueball, smoothed out her apron and leaned towards him.

"Tell me more Cue."

Cueball revisited the days events with Sallie Jean. He continued to reel from the shock and amazement of it all. He started to recall the moonshine Ouida had left on his porch, the busted batch of corn strewn over the Texas Tea, LLC parking lot, the way Patty was cozied up to Kody, Gomer hanging out by processor 3 every day and that slight wiff of alcohol he would catch in the air from time to time.

"Sallie Jean, it was under our noses all along! How in the

world could I have been any more blind. The evidence was right in front of me and yet I never put two and two together!"

"Oh honey, sometimes those closest to situations are the last to really see what actually is going on. You had no way of knowing. Please don't think any more about this. It is not worth beating yourself up over."

Cueball rested his hands in his face and moaned.

"Cue, I know what will help ease the pain you are going through."

"What's that Sallie Jean?"

Sallie Jean leaned over to Cueball and laid the plumpest kiss on his lips taking him to another world far away from the pain of the day.

"Breaker, breaker Papa Bear. You copy?"

"10-4. What's your twenty?"

"I'm over here at the house hidin' all my money in tin cans and plantin' them all over my property."

Sam was a nut. He had lived on that property adjacent to US Highway 59 for years and years. He had a fairly good sized garden and sold fresh produce out of his roadside stand. Let's just say he did sell the stuff he grew but he usually got the rest of his produce from the Mexicans down at the Airline Farmer's Market in Houston. As for hiding his money in tin cans, he was just kidding about that. He was one of those who had a high disdain for the government and therefore did not trust old Uncle Sam nor any bank with his money. He bought pre-paid cards from Walmart and loaded them up so as to keep his business private.

"Well, good for you Veggie Man. What you know good today?"

"Papa Bear, all hell's broke loose over here. I'm surprised you didn't hear all the ruckus on FM1127 down at Tater's shop. FBI and ATF has apparently found out who the major distributor of this moonshine is and who was actually makin' the hooch. Apparently, one of Tater's employees was runnin' that third processor out of her shop durin' the night hours makin' moonshine. Can you believe that! And, to top it off, she was usin' one of Tater's new rigs to ship that shit out each Friday over there to Mr. Emery's marina down by the Livingston Dam."

"To be quite honest, nothin' surprises me down here in the river bottom any more. Gotta go, Momma's hollerin' for me and you know how she is if I don't give her a hand. I'll catch you later Veggie Man."

"Ten-four Papa Bear, over and out."

Dwanna's phone rang and she promptly picked it up.

"What the fuckin', hell!"

"Ouida! I just have to draw the line sometimes with that potty mouth of yours precious one!"

"Dwanna, did you hear Tater goddamn Murphy was makin' moonshine right out of her so-called refinery over there? I knew that business of hers was gunna be more than just an erl re-cyclin' business! And now I know that is the reason she hired my Cue since he has such great business mind when it comes to these type of entremanurial ventures."

"Now, Ouida. First off, the word is 'entrepreneurial' and no that is not exactly how things went down over there. They say they found Coon-Ass Joe's dog Gomer drinking from the spout of one of her processing thingamajigs and he suddenly fell over drunk as a door knob. Apparently, Sheriff Jess and some investigating agent was over there at the time and saw all this happen. They went over and picked up the dog realizing he stunk to high heaven of moonshine. Sheriff Jess and the agent then went over to the spout and both of them took a sip to 'test' the evidence of course. That's when they realized this moonshine deal actually started at Tater's business. They figured out that gal Patty was in on all of this along with one of the drivers that Tater hired to run her rigs. So the agents hauled them all down to Houston for questioning."

"So you mean to tell me that I could have gone straight to Cue rather than havin' to take a cut from my profits by purchasin' that shit from a middleman! What in the mother fuckin' hell is this world comin' to?"

"Ouida Mae, Cue apparently knew nothing about this.

They had some very clever individuals who were able to pull this off behind he and Tater's back. That's about all I know right now but as soon as I hear more, you'll be the first I call."

"Well hell, ain't that the witch's ass. You never can get away with sonofabitchin' nothin' around here. Someone wants to make an honest livin' and not have to pay that muther fucker Uncle Sam and they got that sorry ass FBI/ATF shit makin' sure we poor folks don't get a break. The goddamn American Way!"

Coon-Ass Joe looked over at Ouida and held up his can of Pabst Blue Ribbon.

"I echo dat!"

"Well Ouida, my precious friend, I need to git for now. I'll talk to you later. I love you and Jesus does too."

Ouida sat down next to Coon-Ass Joe, pulled out her flask and threw back the remains inside.

"I just can't believe the crazy shit goin' on in this goddamn town here Joe! What the fuck is gunna happen next? It's just amazin' how folks don't have a mind for nothin' good and don't promote the fuckin' welfare of every sonofabitch all on account of wantin' to get ahead. Let us do what we want with moonshine and stay the hell out of it! It's inexpensive and provides a bit of goodness to those who can't afford the shit they sell down there at the Covered Wagon. Where's the cocksuckin' justice around here? Why the hell does the police need to stick their dicks where they don't belong?"

Coon-Ass Joe turned to her.

"Well, Ouida, ya knows dis dere moonshine stuff is illegal? Ya know dat de law here's de law and they does have a responsibility to uphold it no mattuh whut de benefit dere is fo de po folks round here?"

Joe lifted his left butt cheek off the barstool and ripped a big one damn near gassing out the entire bar. He threw a smirk at Ouida.

"Dat's what I tink of de law!"

HEADLINES

"Lobo! Get in here, I need to read somethin' to you this mornin'!"

Mr. Lobo walked into the kitchen, sat at the bar and motioned that he was ready for whatever his wife had to throw at him. Mrs. Carol read the headlines from the San Jacinto County Times.

"Infamous Multi-Thousand Dollar Moonshine Ring Shut Down."

"Read on Momma."

"Sheriff Jess Murphy, San Jacinto County Sheriff, has been investigating a local moonshine operation since the fall of last year. He brought the FBI and ATF into the investigation once he confirmed the legitimacy of the operation. Multiple business owners were arrested and found guilty of the distribution/sale of moonshine in San Jacinto County. Businesses included The Slots Shack, McMann's Grocery, The Shepherd USPS, The Recycle Center on US 59, Zeke's Drive-In and the Livingston Dam Marina.

Apparently this operation included quite a few underground distributors in the area as well. The main channel was found to be off FM 1127 on Robin Lane. A woman, by the name of Mrs. Belinda Banks, was arrested for harboring the inventory and passing it through bogus UPS channels and other personal drivers. The main break came a few weeks ago when the agents took many of these individuals in for questioning at the FBI headquarters in Houston, Texas. After a lengthy period of questioning, the FBI and ATF determined they would be able to narrow down the investigation by breaking up a local distribution point.

On Thursday morning, January 28, the FBI staked out Mr. Embry's Lake Livingston Dam Marina. One of the agents posed as a UPS driver and was able to subdue Mr. Embry's son, Tank Embry. While the agents posed as fisher folk, Sheriff Jess Murphy approached Mr. Embry to make him aware that he knew of the operation and encouraged him to cooperate with the authorities that morning. Shortly thereafter, a Texas Tea, LLC rig pulled up to disperse moonshine into one of the holding tanks at the marina. Agent Kelly Weems promptly arrested the driver, Kody Lloyd. Mr. Lloyd was employed by Tater Murphy, CEO of Texas Tea, LLC. Mr. Lloyd, as it was discovered later, was also the owner of the bogus UPS trucks and other vehicles that were used in the distribution of the moonshine. Upon inspection of the Lake Livingston Dam Marina warehouse, the agents discovered quite a large moonshine servicing operation. Within the facility they found hoses that tied back to the underground holding tank. The hoses channeled the moonshine through spigots and into mason jars. The filled jars were then loaded into cardboard cases for delivery. Each case was affixed with a label that read "Livingston Dam Marina Motor Oil".

Sheriff Jess Murphy was quoted as saying, 'I don't believe there has been such a unique operation allowing for the preparation of moonshine found in any of the counties in Texas history.'

Later that afternoon, Sheriff Murphy and a host of ATF and FBI agents raided Texas Tea, LLC. Upon arrival they handcuffed Tabitha 'Tater' Murphy, Johnny 'Cueball' Whitehead, Patricia 'Patty' Dunstan and Marvin Marks.

Sheriff Murphy discovered Gomer, Coon-Ass Joe James' dog, roaming the Texas Tea, LLC yard drunker than a cooter brown. He and one of the FBI agents discovered the dog had been licking the remnants of moonshine from a spigot of the third refining processor on the property. Further evidence suggests the moonshine was being made on site because of the corn kernels that were strewn throughout the parking lot and processing area.

After questioning those on the premises, Ms. Murphy and Mr. Jones' handcuffs were removed as the FBI strongly believed they were in no way connected with the operation. Marvin Marks, database administrator for Texas Tea, LLC, was the mastermind behind the operation. He, Ms. Dunstand and Mr. Lloyd were close friends. They had both attended Spring High

School together and maintained their friendship over the years. When Mr. Marks was recruited by Ms. Murphy to set up the technology infrastructure for Texas Tea, LLC, he called Ms. Dunstan to be on the lookout for a job opening at the new company. Once Ms. Dunstan was hired on, she contacted Mr. Lloyd and recommended he be on the lookout for a rig driver job there. She had informed Mr. Lloyd of the potential business plan she had in mind to make them both a bit of cash on the side.

Ms. Murphy had set up a new, third processor on the premises to serve as a backup to the other two in operation hoping to eventually expand the business. Ultimately, Ms. Dunstan determined this processor could be utilized in the interim as a distillery for moonshine. Ms. Dunstan had previously worked at St. Arnold's Brewery in Houston, Texas as one of the intern brewmasters. She apparently understood the art of distilling well enough to contribute to the mastermind scheme. Mr. Lloyd ingeniously configured processor number three on a separate server that routed directly to his office in The Woodlands, Texas ensuring no one was aware that it was actually being used at all. Ms. Dunstan was able to gain the respect of both Tater Murphy and Johnny 'Cueball' Whitehead in order that they trust her with opening the shop every morning. What this allowed for was Ms. Dunstan, Mr. Lloyd and Mr. Marks to take deliveries of moonshine distilling supplies during the early morning hours and use those late night hours to actually brew the white lightning. Once the moonshine was distilled, Ms. Dunstan would open the yard up early in the morning, every Friday, to allow Mr. Lloyd to fill up the Texas Tea, LLC rig that had not been released into operation yet. He would then drive the rig to the Lake Livingston Dam Marina and fill one of their empty fuel tanks with moonshine later to be jarred, boxed and distributed by Mr. Embry and his son Tank.

Agents also confiscated a safe containing a number of pre-paid Walmart Visa cards at Mr. Mark's office in The Woodlands, Texas. They discovered each were loaded with an average of five thousand dollars totaling one million dollars overall. It appears the operation spanned San Jacinto County as well as neighboring Polk, Walker and Trinity counties. Over 25 people were involved in either the manufacturing, distribution or sale of moonshine over the past several months. Some have received lesser sentences based on their testimony. Ms. Ouida Lawless, daughter of former Mayor Harold Lawless, received an adjudicated sentence based on her assistance in helping both the FBI and ATF in their investigation. The average time spent by most of the offenders will be five to ten years. The upcoming trial of Mr. Marks, Mr. Lloyd and Ms. Dunstan, who have been indicted by a federal grand jury in Houston for allegedly conspiring in a moonshine racketeering enterprise, will include possible convictions for the offenses of engaging in the distillation of moonshine, engaging in tax fraud by the distiller, engaging in the distribution of moonshine, engaging in money laundering as well as the possession of sawed off shotguns all in attempt to defraud the United States of America.

Lawyers for the defendants have no comment at this time. This was announced by the U.S. Attorney of the Southern District of Texas, D. Sims. The investigation was lead by our own Sheriff Jess Murphy as well as Special Agent in Charge Kelly Weems of the Bureau of Alcohol, Tobacco, Firearms and Explosives (ATF) Houston Division and FBI Special Agent in Charge Frank Horton of the Houston Field Office. The ATF and FBI extend their thanks to the local community for their assistance in the investigation including Ms. Dwanna Crabb, Mr. and Mrs. Bobby 'Lobo' Fuller, Mr. Clyde Betts and Mr. Samuel Green."

"Well, how about that Momma. Wonder if we will get a moonshiner medal of honor?"

Mr. Murphy and Mr. Lobo met up at the Feed Store the following week and commenced to solving more of the world's problems. The exception this day was Murphy had been so preoccupied with the events of the past couple of weeks he hadn't had a platform to voice his frustration. Texas Tea, L.L.C had been closed down for a month due to the investigation, inventory, confiscation of rig number five and the third processing unit. None of which were going to be given back to

Tater. Mr. Murphy considered this a minimal loss to the business, considering the circumstances. The bright side was, however, the investors had called he and Tater into a special meeting and told them the entire fiasco was shocking yet they were proud of Tater for the way she handled things. They were going to front the money to add back a third unit and tanker but first wanted to see Tater take a vacation and recover from everything that had occurred. They sent her off to Ambergris Caye, Belize to spend some time fishing, sailing and sunning at her long time friends, Lucy Ruth and Ghetto Girl's condo. This was her favorite place on earth other than Shepherd, Texas and she was extremely happy for the distraction.

Tater returned refreshed and focused. She and Cueball immediately began setting up the new equipment. Tater brought on Mr. Lobo's daughter to help her with the technical configuration and to maintain the database and cloud servers going forward. The company was back up and running in no time. Over the next year she was able to expand her business, kick off operation on processor number three, add another new rig and begin plans for expanding her business to additional territories within the next fiscal year. She and her daddy couldn't be happier. The legend of the Moonshine take-down would forever be part of their moral fiber and a story that Tater and her daddy, as well as the inhabitants of the River Bottom, would tell for generations to come.

So you see, there's always something brewing down here in the River Bottom. So many lives going to waste over stupid business dealings. Had they used their brilliant imaginations for more reputable efforts, there would be quite a few multi-millionaires living in this county. The moonshiner legacy of San Jacinto County helps outsiders understand a bit better what it is to live down here in the River Bottom. There are more stories to share of this beautifully enchanted mischievous place. There are equally as many opportunities to hang out with one another and solve the world's problems.

PROLOGUE

Incurable ailments around the county have left no hope for many of those battling illnesses. A new entrepreneurial enterprise rises up in an effort to combat these challenges and sends Sheriff Jess and company on yet another search to unravel the newest mystery to hit the surrounding area.

Dwanna has inherited a business from her dearly departed parents and finds a new lease on life as well as a new outlet to reach others on behalf of her sweet Jesus. Along the way she stumbles into a love affair with a new gentleman in town which creates discord between she and Ouida.

Cue and Sallie Jean grow closer together only to find that heartbreak soon threatens them. Tater steps in to support the two in the hopes that things turn around.

Ouida encounters the shock of her life taking her through an incredible journey.

What is at the heart of this new mystery? Who finds themselves in muddy water this time? What happens to one of the beloved? All of this and more to be uncovered in the upcoming book . . . Anointing Oil.

About Debra Fuller

I'm a native Texan born and raised in the Houston metropolitan area. Most of my childhood was spent in my ever-evolving imagination. I loved lying in the cool green grass of my grandmother's backyard, staring up at the sky while conversing with my invisible friend Johnny.

I have always loved reading. Books are my escape route from the concerns of life transporting me to another world.

My influence in storytelling was my Daddy. I spent many years sitting on his back porch listening to his stories about work, family and life. Many of those porch moments were focused on solving the world's problems. My stories are influenced also by my experiences in East Texas, the people I have met and the various circumstances that I have encountered.

My intent is to take you on a diversion from your daily concerns hoping to provide you with an outlet to laugh, cry, scream and even cuss a little with the characters brought to life in my series.

Made in the USA
Coppell, TX
15 July 2023

19199425R00152